"Does the storm frighten you?"

he asked softly.

"No," she said in a small voice, noting how the occasional bursts of light outside the window outlined his solid frame. But when a crash of thunder sounded, nearer than before, she instinctively reached for him, taking comfort in the strength of his muscular forearm beneath the soft wool wrap.

Unexpectedly, the lights came on again. Meera blushed, her hand still on his arm, her body nestled close to his. Then, too late, she realized that he was staring down at her hand. . .her *left* hand!

Elliot was stone cold—as cold as the wet breeches clinging to his legs. His gaze was locked on the hard object that glittered like cold fire on her finger.

"Well, I see you've made your decision," he said blandly, his unemotional tone belying the ache in his heart.

YVONNE LEHMAN is an award-winning novelist and founder of the Blue Ridge Christian Writers Conference, for many years held annually at the Blue Ridge Assembly in Black Mountain, North Carolina, which serves as the enchanting setting for this, her tenth published novel.

She is listed in *Who's Who of America, Personalities of the South, Contemporary Authors,* and the *International Authors & Writers Who's Who,* among others.

Yvonne also teaches at a local university, and is a wife, mother, and grandmother, residing with her husband in Black Mountain, where she helps daughter Lorie run a silk flower shop in her spare time!

Books by Yvonne Lehman

HEARTSONG PRESENTS
HP37—Drums of Shelomoh
HP82—Southern Gentleman

Mountain Man

Yvonne Lehman

Heartsong Presents

To Steve and Cindy

A note from the Author:
I love to hear from my readers! You may write to me at
the following address: **Yvonne Lehman**
Author Relations
P.O. Box 719
Uhrichsville, OH 44683

ISBN 1-55748-663-8

MOUNTAIN MAN

Cover illustration by Brian Bowman.

PRINTED IN THE U.S.A.

one

"Do I dare?"

The question rolled around like thunder in Meera Briskin's head as she watched the lightning skitter across the midnight sky, shimmering above the forest. Outside her third-floor bedroom window, the clashing of the elements reminded her of the heated exchange earlier.

Family members had gathered at the mountaintop estate—a majestic brick mansion with great white columns—to honor the memory of Elias Briskin on the one-year anniversary of his death. And rather naturally, the conversation had turned to the selling of a piece of property they had jointly inherited from him.

"You can't be serious about selling to a developer," Meera had protested. "They might build a shopping center or condos across the top of the mountain."

"Humph! That's not our concern," an uncle had declared.

"Of course it is," Meera had countered, glancing at her dad who looked thoughtful but did not come to her defense. "We need to think of the beauty of North Carolina's Blue Ridge Mountains. And we have to consider the environment."

"Oh, really, Meera," her cousin Louisa snorted. "There you go with another of your do-gooder projects! Ever since you took a few environmental courses, you think everybody is out to pollute the atmosphere. You did the same thing when you studied nutrition. Suddenly, we were all condemned for eating junk food and animal fat."

Laughter followed, not unkindly, but as a show of appreciation for Louisa's theatrics. Meera hadn't attempted a defense. She'd grown accustomed to her cousin's tactless jabs. She took a deep breath, and with her pulse beating like the rain against the windowpanes, she'd plunged in before she lost her nerve. "We could at least inform the Maxwells about a possible sale."

Stunned silence fell upon the little group gathered in the drawing room.

"The land adjoins their property, you know," Meera continued. They stared in stark disbelief. "It's only fair. . . ." Her voice trailed off and she lowered her gaze from the unsympathetic faces of her family.

"Really, Meera," Louisa rebutted, "the Maxwells never cared about the environment. They built Chestnut Lodge smack-dab on top of the mountain. And they never cared about human life either." Her next words were ominous, throbbing against the background of the rumbling thunder. "Or have you forgotten that old man Maxwell tried to *kill* our grandfather?"

"Stop it!" came Aunt Clara's sharp reprimand. "That name should not be spoken in this house."

"I'm sorry," Meera apologized. It *was* regrettable if anyone thought her disloyal to her beloved grandfather's memory. But she also had her conscience to deal with. "I can't give my consent to sell without further thought."

Later that night, Louisa had come into Meera's bedroom and approached the subject again. "Look, Meera, I don't mean to be unpleasant," she said, sitting in the middle of the bed in her babydoll pajamas. "This might sound selfish, but Gramps did leave a share of the land to me and, frankly, I want the money." She waved her hands dismissively. "Let the big shots decide what to build on the mountain and whether or not it's harmful to the environment. Goodness knows, *I* can't do anything about it."

Meera began to brush her silver-blond hair and watched her vivacious, dark-haired cousin reflected in the mirror as she talked.

"You know, Meera, the decision to sell doesn't need to be unanimous. If the rest of us agree, we don't need *your* consent. And who's to say the Maxwells wouldn't do something worse than the developers anyway?" Louisa added earnestly.

"Like I said, Louisa," Meera put in, eager to ease the tension between them—tension that had originated not with the discussion of the property sale, but with a more personal matter, "I'll think about it."

"Well, think fast," retorted the disgruntled Louisa as she jumped off the bed and strode from the room.

Meera switched off the light and stood at the window, watching the intermittent light flashing like a distress signal in the spring sky. She had "thought fast" when she'd flung the engagement ring at Clark Phillips after she'd caught him responding to Louisa's outrageous flirtations. But when he told her she was making a mountain out of a molehill, she had been persuaded to put the ring back on her finger.

That incident—and the deep-rooted hostility between the Briskins and Maxwells—were not matters she should "think fast" about. She had dared mention the name of Maxwell to her family and the result had been alienating. She had dared to become engaged to Clark Phillips, and she had to admit she might have been mistaken. If she dared do what she was considering now, the repercussions could be. . .disastrous.

Meera knew the biblical injunction to love your neighbor—but it also said something about not casting "pearls before swine." How was she to know which Scripture to obey? Or was she simply expected to perpetuate the feud that had begun three generations ago and now seemed to be her legacy to pass on to future generations?

A loud crash of thunder jolted her from her reverie.

Or maybe it was her sudden jarring decision. Yes! In all good conscience, she must find out for herself whether or not the Maxwells were decent human beings who deserved to know about the property sale, or if, in fact, they were unmitigated scoundrels who should remain her bitter enemies to the death.

The question was—if she did anything—what would it be? And how would she do it?

Where there's a will, there's a way, she reminded herself, glancing over at her purse which held a particular writers' conference brochure. Yes, she knew of a way; she just didn't know if she dared pursue it.

❧

By morning Meera had decided that the only place to really think was in the solitude of her grandfather's hunting lodge. With a stab of loneliness, she realized that it was *her* cabin now. He had left it to her, along with a small section of land adjoining Turkey Creek.

She put on some shorts and a sleeveless shirt, rolled the top down on her convertible, and left the big house. Fluffy white clouds dotted the gray-blue sky, washed clean by the rain and rose-stained by the early sun just peeking over the mountains.

The wind blew her hair back from her face and the scent of fresh earth and pine filled her nostrils. The car dipped into the shadowed forest. Her descent along the paved one-lane road curving down the back side of the mountain led her to the dirt road running alongside the creek, swollen now from the previous night's storm.

Meera could almost see herself and her cousin Louisa as children, wading and splashing on the Briskin side of Turkey

Creek, singing at the top of their lungs, "Feudin', a-fussin', and a-fightin'. Sometimes, it gets downright excitin'."

Time and again, their boisterous melody had lifted like the morning mist rising from the forest floor to meet the sun at break of day. The sound had reverberated around the mountainsides and bounced back at them like an approving chorus, echoing, "Citin'. . .citin'. . .citin'."

Those days had been exciting! The Briskin-Maxwell feud had provided the impetus for their greatest fears and sparked their imaginations as to how they might conquer the Maxwell monsters. It had infiltrated their daily life and was incorporated into most of their childhood games.

In a race, the last one home was not a rotten egg—but a Maxwell.

When it rained while the sun was shining, it wasn't the devil beating his wife—it was a Maxwell.

In a fight, the nastiest word one child could call another was—*Maxwell*.

Such memories weren't exciting anymore; rather, disturbing. Meera parked the silver car beside the log cabin, got out, and surveyed the place so close to her heart, acutely conscious of familiar mountain sounds. She'd missed them. The creek singing over the rocks. The birds chirping their greeting to the day. Small animals scurrying about their woodland chores.

She hadn't visited the cabin in over a year, not since her grandfather's death. Now, as she stepped up on the porch, her heart was heavy. Grandfather Elias had purposely built this cabin from blighted chestnut wood, deliberately facing Maxwell property. Maxwells would not listen to anything a Briskin had to say, so this was his mute statement. He had nothing to hide—nothing to be ashamed of. Her grandfather had wanted only peace, but Maxwells were not receptive to that message.

Meera had inherited not only the cabin, but the blighted legacy of discordant families. For the moment, however, determined to face whatever memories awaited her inside, she stooped down and took a key from under the mat. Then she opened the front screen, unlocked the door, and went inside.

She was not quite prepared for the stunning emotions that met her when she crossed the hardwood floor and looked around at the golden chestnut walls and the old stone fireplace. Tears came to her eyes. She and her grandfather had spent some wonderful times here together.

She felt an overwhelming sense of his presence as she walked through the familiar rooms. Seeing his rocking chair, she recalled the times she'd crawled into his lap during a storm and felt his protective arms around her. Walking over to his bed, she trailed her hand across the patchwork quilt he had liked so much. It was a double wedding ring pattern, quilted by the grandmother she'd never known, except for her grandfather's description. On the bedside table was his Bible that had been his guidebook for living.

In the kitchen Meera plugged in the empty refrigerator and it began to hum. Her eyes roamed over the hardwood table. Then she went to the window over the sink to look out at the slope of the wooded mountainside behind the cabin.

Walking back to the bedroom she always used, she twisted the ring from her finger and held it in the palm of her hand. Clark had said that after she had a little time to think, he wanted her to return to Venezuela and make a more serious, lasting commitment to their relationship. They were meant for each other, he'd said. That's what she'd thought too. . .at first. Then she'd had some niggling doubts. Now, back in her own territory, she was less sure than ever.

Suddenly, the sound of a chain saw startled her from her thoughts. She put the ring on the bedside table, hurried into the living room, and looked out the window.

Four men in waders were working farther downstream. Her gaze wandered to the shotgun above the mantel and back toward the men. But upon closer inspection, she could see that they were removing part of a huge oak, apparently split by lightning during last night's storm. The fallen portion lay across the swollen creek. The men, working from the Maxwell side of the creek, were having difficulty removing the limbs. She wondered if they dared not trespass on Briskin property.

Several yards away stood a blackened tree trunk, sheared off halfway down. That would have to be felled.

She didn't know if the men working in the creek were Maxwells or their hired hands. She did know that across the creek, on the Maxwell side, her grandfather had been shot, a friendship had ended, and the feud had intensified between the two families.

She'd grown up to despise the name of Maxwell, yet she'd only occasionally glimpsed them on the opposite side of the property line. And only once in her life had she even stuck her big toe in the Maxwell half of Turkey Creek, and that action had caused her to fall smack on her bottom.

Meera turned back into the room and lit a fire to dispel the dampness. The sun wouldn't reach the cabin before mid-morning. After the men left, she would open the windows to air out the musty cabin. That was time enough to begin some serious cleaning.

For now, she sat in her grandfather's big worn recliner and stared into the fire. "I wish you were here to advise me, Grandfather," she said aloud to the cabin, so full of him, yet so empty without him.

She could not feel the comfort of his loving arms around her but knew what he'd say if he were here. He'd taken his philosophy straight from the Scriptures: "I will lift up my eyes unto the hills; from there comes my help."

Meera knew he had been referring to God. But whenever she stood on the porch, held onto the banister, gazed beyond the rippling creek, and lifted her eyes to the hills. . .they were Maxwell hills.

She again thought about the brochure Cathy Steinbord had given her when she'd visited with her in the valley a couple of days ago. Although she and Cathy weren't close friends, they had a common bond. They were both natives of this area and both had studied journalism together at Chapel Hill.

The famous Trevor Steinbord, Cathy's brother, would be the banquet speaker on the final night of the conference. If Meera acted upon the idea that still rumbled like a spring storm in her head—attending that conference—it wouldn't be entirely a farce. She did have a degree in journalism! She'd even had several travel and food articles published! Besides, she really would like to discover if she had real writing ability—particularly now that she had doubts about becoming Mrs. Clark Phillips.

The conference would be held this coming week at Chestnut Lodge, owned by the Maxwell family, and located, as Louisa had said, "Smack-dab on top of Maxwell Mountain."

A song Meera had sung years ago in Sunday school came to mind: "Dare to be a Daniel." The story was a familiar one. When the prophet Daniel was thrown into the lions' den, God had shut the lions' mouths, and he had escaped unharmed. But Daniel had been forced there, she mused; he hadn't gone in willingly and tempted fate.

Regardless, the gooseflesh rose on Meera's arms, and she felt the tingle of excitement. It was the most adventurous thing she'd ever considered undertaking. Would she? Should she? Could she? Just as the chain saw stopped buzzing, so did the jumble of thoughts in her head. Suddenly she knew the answer.

Yes! She would dare! She would venture into forbidden Maxwell territory. It might be worth the risk.

two

A week after she made the decision—one she hoped wouldn't prove to be fatal—Meera felt she was ready for the most daring adventure of her life. To make the whole thing more legitimate, she had called the editor of *Fabulous Places*, for whom she'd written several articles, and had gotten his approval to write a series on noteworthy inns of western North Carolina.

Chestnut Lodge was, as the locals said, only "a hop, a skip, and a jump" from her home. And if she didn't have to do this incognito, she could simply walk across the creek, tramp through the forest, and hike up the mountain.

Needing to conceal her identity, however, Meera drove the long way around via the Blue Ridge Parkway where the mountains met the sky. If the lodge looked anything like the picture on the brochure, it would be an impressive place. In summer, the foliage was much too lush for her to be able to see the complex, but in the winter, when the trees were bare, she had glimpsed lights twinkling high on Maxwell Mountain. With the coldest weather behind, the trees were awakening, trembling with tender young leaves. Maples, bursting with new life, sported red buds. Willows swayed golden in the sunlight, and dogwood blossoms, fragile as a whisper, looked like white butterflies flitting on the mountainsides.

She felt them in her stomach when she actually turned onto the exit marked with a green sign, bold white letters proclaiming, "Chestnut Lodge." After traveling for a while along Biltmore Avenue, Meera turned onto Maxwell property and began the ascent up the mountain, feeling much as she had felt that time she'd flown in a small plane all the way to Hawaii. She'd hung onto her seat for dear life. . .as she was holding onto the steering wheel now. Then and now, she reminded herself, she was at one of those points of no return, so she might as well relax.

The road forked at the entrance to Chestnut Lodge. Now she couldn't turn around—even if she wanted to—without considerable difficulty. Concentrating on every detail of the drive, she tucked away the information she would need if she were to accomplish her purpose.

For more than a mile, the narrow paved road was bordered by great pines whose branches intertwined like giant fingers to form a green arch overhead. Younger pines grew between the large ones and Meera could appreciate the obvious planning for future growth, when the older pines would be replaced.

Before long, she came upon a section that was wild and natural, reminding her of Briskin property. At two different places along the curving road, a tumbling creek was spanned by expertly erected stone bridges.

Then, she was once again winding over the road beneath spreading pine branches that exuded a fresh, fragrant scent. The road turned into a long concrete incline bordered by low stone walls in which were set pink and white flowering dogwoods, thick rhododendron, and yellow blooming forsythia. Myriads of white and yellow daffodils, like welcoming miniature trumpets, swayed on green stems.

Suddenly there it was. Crowning the mountain amid a thicket of lush evergreens and great maples, oaks, and poplars was a three-story white structure beneath a gray slate shingled roof studded with chimneys.

Meera knew that the hub of the lodge had once been the

Maxwell family residence, decorated in a restrained Queen Ann style, with thirty rooms and many fireplaces. Surprisingly, her grandfather had spoken of the place appreciatively, though the Maxwell taste in architecture had differed from his own. The Briskin mansion was an expression of modern elegance—a three-story brick with great white columns and a lower level that boasted a gymnasium and heated swimming pool.

Meera parked at the side of the drive, near the entrance, then walked to the edge of a cliff, where a waist-high stone wall formed a protective railing. From here the view was spectacular. The drive over, made in early-morning shadows, had not prepared her for the effect of the sun bursting upon the lush rolling hills and valleys, transforming them into a green-gold wonderland.

At one time or another, Meera had visited all the lodges, inns, and castles in the area—except this one. Biltmore House and gardens was in a class by itself. Grove Park Inn was a masterpiece carved in stone. The unique architecture of the Assembly Inn at Montreat reminded her of a medieval castle. Then there was Pisgah Inn and Black Forest Lodge. She could have named more. Having been brought up in this area, she was familiar with all of them.

But this one—not as grand as some, larger than others—compared favorably with other inns. She had seen pictures, of course, and had read about it. But Chestnut Lodge itself had been off limits. Now she was here and could see for herself.

Turning back toward the lodge, Meera reminded herself that she had every right to be here. After all, it was open to the public, she was paying her own way, and she meant no harm. With that resolve, and ignoring the gooseflesh that prickled up and down her arms, she opened the massive glass doors, marched across the marble floor of the lobby, and zeroed in on her destination—the registration desk.

She stood waiting for the next available clerk, then signed in as "Meera Brown." It wasn't exactly a lie. She'd used that pen name on the few published articles she'd written.

"Any Maxwells around?" she asked, careful not to trip over the name.

"Always!" The clerk, a curly-headed young man with a friendly face, chuckled.

Not wanting to betray her interest in the Maxwells, Meera began asking about the conference beginning that afternoon.

"There's the man who can answer your questions." Glancing over her shoulder, the clerk lifted his hand to hail someone. "Sir!" he called just as a thud sounded from behind her and she turned to see what had caused it.

"Be right with you, Tom," came a masculine voice.

The man, dressed in a suit and tie, bent to retrieve a box that had fallen from a cart onto the floor, and with the sudden exertion, Meera couldn't help noticing the straining of taut muscles against the dark fabric of his suit coat. Being a physical fitness enthusiast herself, she could appreciate the discipline required to keep one's body toned and fit. She also noticed the man's air of firm authority in cautioning the young employee who had been unloading the boxes. This man was obviously someone in charge—the conference director, maybe, or a faculty member.

While she waited, Meera lifted her gaze to the the octagonal-shaped ceiling, dominated by a great crystal chandelier hanging from the center. Fans on chestnut crossbeams droned softly. She was acutely conscious of the paneled walls made of now-extinct golden American chestnut paneling and a magnificent wide staircase that rose three stories high, from which one could look down into the elegant, yet cozy lobby with its furniture groupings, its fine thick rugs, lush plants, and huge stone fireplace.

Over the fireplace hung a painting that caught her eye. It was a forest scene—no doubt depicting the chestnuts when they were alive and well—*when all was well between the Briskins and the Maxwells,* she added mentally.

What am I doing here? Meera thought and felt an urge to escape, to forget this ridiculous idea of hers. She shifted the straps of her bag from her hand to her shoulder. Instinct told her to return the room key to the desk clerk and make a hasty departure.

However, the man Tom had hailed was now striding her way in the manner of one accustomed to walking up and down mountains so that on level ground it seemed almost too easy. He was tall, with the muscular build and take-charge aura she had already noted.

As he approached, he glanced at Tom, who gestured toward Meera. "Miss Brown would like a word with you."

Although the man's eyes held a trace of admiration as his deep blue gaze shifted from the desk clerk to her, Meera was conscious of her casual attire—denim shorts, T-shirt, and wind-blown strands of hair that had worked their way free of the confining knot on top of her head. Unaccountably, she wished she had taken more pains with her appearance.

Smiling, she extended her hand to the attractive man whose dark wavy hair, neatly trimmed, topped a ruggedly handsome face. Maybe her task here wouldn't be so bad, after all. She could observe the Maxwells from a distance while making new friends and developing her writing skills. "You're here for the conference?"

His voice was pleasantly husky. "For the duration," he replied and reached for her hand. "I'm Elliot Maxwell." The sun glinted in his eyes and the rest of his greeting was lost on her.

Meera tried to withdraw her small hand, but it was en-gulfed in his large one. She'd never before touched a Max-well. She had supposed the sensation would be something like holding a frog, that she'd get warts or something. But it was warmth she felt—not warts—traveling from her hand and into her arm before a hot blush flooded her face.

He must have felt her tremble, for he gave her hand a firm shake, then released it.

It wasn't easy, making the transition from finding an at-tractive man appealing, to realizing that he was supposed to be her mortal enemy. This man was a Maxwell! She had to do something—say something. "Could I have a word with you? I mean. . ."

"Certainly," he said with a devastatingly charming smile and gestured toward a door near the entrance. "We can talk in my office."

She hadn't meant to do it this way. Not dressed like a high-schooler. And not stuttering and stammering like a ninny! She had thought she was prepared to invade Maxwell turf. But meeting one of them in the flesh had unnerved her more than she might have suspected, and she mentally kicked herself for being caught off guard.

Besides, she had thought all the Maxwells were old, and this man couldn't be much more than thirty. She supposed her assumption had been based on childhood impressions. She'd never seen a child on the Maxwell side of Turkey Creek. Only on rare occasions had she even glimpsed one of the adults walking in their part of the woods.

Inside the room—more like a cozy den than an office—Meera stepped into an even greater reminder that she was an intruder. The sun, streaming through the windows, had turned the chestnut walls to gold. How appropriate, she thought rue-fully. The chestnut trees had been like gold to the Maxwells once—before the blight that had started the feud between her family and his.

She needed air. Abruptly Meera walked across to the open windows and inhaled deeply of the cool mountain breeze, filled with the fragrance of pine and warm, moist humus. Her gaze fell upon the nearest mountaintop that belonged to her family, and she was reminded of her purpose here. Reminded that a developer wanted to buy that mountain, shave off the top, and build condos—or worse, a shopping center. The appeal of Chestnut Lodge would then be threatened.

Honesty forced her to admit, however, that this was not her primary reason for being here. She could have had an attorney inform the Maxwells about the sale. Wasn't she really trying to be the first Briskin to make peace? After all, she had no quarrel with these people. Or was she merely trying to satisfy her curiosity? *Curiosity killed the cat,* she thought.

Why couldn't she just turn around and say, "I'm Meera Briskin and I want to give you the opportunity to buy our mountain—to preserve the beauty of these forests and to protect our environment"? Why? *Why, my foot! That kind of offer is what started the blasted feud in the first place.*

Thus justifying her little deceit, she squared her shoulders and turned to face Elliot Maxwell. Her gray eyes couldn't quite meet his blue ones this time. Instead, she glanced around and said the first thing that came to mind. "This is the most beautiful wood I've ever seen."

He smiled his approval at the compliment and motioned her toward an easy chair by the fireplace. She sat and crossed her long, slender legs, concentrating on the green peace lilies with their white blooms, standing in brass pots in front of the fireplace.

"Genuine American chestnut," Elliot said proudly. "There's no wood like this anymore." An expression of sadness crossed his handsome features. "Every American chestnut tree has been destroyed—gone forever. But you may know all about that. Are you from this area?"

She would be as honest as she could. "My parents have a home in Charlotte," she said but did not mention the one on the French Riviera or their joint ownership of the Briskin estate.

Meera had read the historical account of the chestnut blight. She knew the Briskin version of how the blight had sabotaged not only the trees but the Briskin-Maxwell friendship. But she had not heard the Maxwell version. And since there were always two sides to every story, she was willing to listen to what Elliot Maxwell had to say.

She glanced over at him and saw that his eyes followed the movement of her hand as she unconsciously traced a pattern with her room key along the denim of her shorts, a few inches above her knees. Then their eyes met and she put her hands in her lap.

Moistening her lips, she plunged in. "That's one reason I'm here. I'm interested in doing some research and writing an article about Chestnut Lodge."

He broke into a wide smile. "That's what you wanted to talk to me about?"

She nodded, not comprehending his attitude.

"That's a relief. I thought you had a problem with our establishment. You seemed so uncertain. . .reluctant. . ."

"Well. . .I was a little hesitant to ask you about this," Meera admitted, thinking fast. "And I hadn't intended to do it just yet. This is hardly a professional approach." She glanced down at her bare legs and wrinkled her nose.

"Perhaps not," he replied, sobering, and her heart did a quick flip. "Perhaps not professional, Miss Brown. . .but you *have* caught my attention. And I must confess, normally I would have turned down such a request by now."

But he hadn't. And seeing a flicker of genuine interest in his eyes, she heard herself asking, "So, you've heard this line before?"

"Probably," he said matter-of-factly. "Probably as many times as you've heard that you're a strikingly beautiful woman."

Meera's breath caught in her throat. Yes, she'd heard it and had never failed to be pleased. But she had never expected to hear it from a Maxwell. And if she had, she would never have expected to like it. Then why this sudden elation? Why this feeling of having received the ultimate compliment?

This was madness! She should not be sitting here, smiling at a Maxwell, enjoying his company. "Then. . ." she pressed, realizing she might never have this opportunity again, "does this mean yes?"

He laughed, and again she was stirred by the sound of his pleasure. "It means I will take the matter under consideration, Miss Brown. That is," he paused, uncrossing his legs and placing his hands on the arms of his chair, "if we could proceed on a first name basis."

"Meera," she said as his desk phone rang.

He rose to answer it and quickly turned toward the window, then glanced back at her while he listened. He replied in a few unrevealing words and turned away again, but not before she detected a look of sheer frustration in his eyes. His lips thinned and his squared chin now seemed to jut forward slightly.

"Yes, I'll be out in a moment," he finished and hung up.

Meera stood. Her emotions ran rampant. She desperately wanted to be honest with Elliot Maxwell. But to confess that she was a Briskin would result in her being thrown out of Chestnut Lodge without having accomplished anything—except to add fuel to the flame of the family feud. "I've taken up enough of your time," she apologized and moved toward the door.

"Just a second." Elliot walked around the desk and leaned back against the edge, arms folded across his chest. "We were interrupted. Did you say your name is Mirror. . .as in looking glass?"

She laughed lightly and spelled it for him. "M-e-e-r-a. It's a family name. My great-great-grandmother. I think it has something to do with the sea."

"Unusual," he murmured. "Is that your car out front? The silver convertible?"

"Yes. Is it blocking traffic or something? Was that what the phone call. . . ?"

"No, no," he said, dismissing her concern with a wave of his hand, though she sensed something different in his mood. "Your car is in the unloading zone," he was saying, "but traffic's not backed up out there. You're okay for a while. But we will talk again. . .Meera."

છ

Yes, Elliot was thinking as he stared at the door that closed softly behind her, they would talk again! She had stirred something in him. . .curiosity, fascination, perhaps even a gnawing suspicion. Perhaps there was a reason for that feeling of deja vu that had come over him when he'd seen her standing in the lobby.

With a quick movement, Elliot reached for the phone and punched out a couple of intercom numbers. "Tom, pick up, please."

"Yes, Mr. Maxwell?"

"Send someone out to get the license plate numbers on that silver convertible in front. . .discreetly. . .and get back to me as soon as possible."

Elliot hoped, with all his might, that this would prove not

to be an act of condemnation, but an act of acquittal.

ஃ

Elliot crumpled the slip of paper in his fist, wishing he could as easily dismiss the thought of the numbers he had written down.

He shouldn't be standing in the shadows beside the front window, spying on that beautiful long-legged girl while a bellman helped with her luggage. But his suspicions had been aroused the moment he'd heard the name. The only Meera he'd ever heard of was a. . .Briskin!

When she had introduced herself, the name had triggered a startling memory. Years ago, after spring rains, he'd gone with his dad to check out damage to the mountain. A giant pine had snapped and dammed up the creek that snaked across Briskin and Maxwell land. Briskin men were at work removing the tree.

Elliot had seen a young girl, probably just barely into her teens, wading in the creek. Thick silver pigtails hung down the front of her shirt, and her face was a delicate oval with enormous eyes that reflected the color of the Carolina gray-blue sky.

He'd been twenty-two then, and not at all interested in the tall, lanky girl who'd stared at him as if he were an alien. The only expectation he had of Briskins was that they stay on their side of the property line.

Then to his surprise, she had raised her hands to her ears, waggled her fingers, and stuck out her tongue. He had reached down to pick up a rock. He'd had no intention of throwing it, but it had served its purpose, for she had turned and tried to run. Then, before he knew it, she had slipped and fallen with a tremendous splash into the rushing water.

An involuntary laugh had escaped Elliot's lips, and he had instinctively reached out to help.

"Don't you dare touch me!" she had screeched just as a man called, "Mirror!" And she had shot Elliot a murderous look before rising awkwardly, sopping wet, and sploshed huffily to the bank.

"Don't worry, 'Mirror'! I wouldn't touch you with a ten-foot pole!" he'd called out, laughing at her discomfort.

At the time he had thought it a strange name—"Mirror." And he hadn't seen it again until years later when he read it in the newspaper. The name was not "Mirror," but "Meera." A picture of a pretty face surrounded by a cloud of hair like sunlight, along with an engagement announcement, confirmed that she had grown up.

He'd seen the name Meera one other time—in old man Briskin's obituary, where she was listed as a grandchild.

Now Meera Briskin—or Brown—was a guest at his lodge. She couldn't be the same. Meera Briskin could go to a writers' conference anywhere in the world. She could certainly afford it. The Briskins had made their fortune by cheating the Maxwells out of theirs!

So what was she doing here? And why use a fake name? Or was it? Had she married a Brown? The tumultuous thoughts bathed his forehead in sweat and he clenched his fists. She'd called herself "Miss." Or had Tom used that term? She wasn't wearing an engagement ring or wedding band. And the challenge he thought he'd seen in her eyes did not send the message, "Don't touch!"

In fact . . .

No! He mustn't fall for this. It was the ploy of a Briskin three generations back. *They pretended to be friendly, then stabbed you in the back.* He didn't want to think about that feud, nor did he want to perpetuate it. All he wanted was for them to stay on their side of the creek, and he'd stay on his.

Still, it appeared that another trouble-making Briskin was

up to something. Fortunately for him, she hadn't used a fake *first* name. He had to know. As much as he hated such an underhanded act, he had no choice. He owed it to his family, his establishment, and his own peace of mind.

All afternoon, he had toyed with the idea of running the license number by a friend of his on the police force. He picked up the phone and called Joe Angel and called out the digits on the crumpled piece of paper, smudged from his damp palm, and asked him to check out the registration.

When he turned again toward the window, Meera and the silver convertible had disappeared. He had a hotel to run, a conference director to greet, a million things to do—but it had to wait. One impossible young woman had turned his orderly world upside down.

Impatiently, he paced. Crossing the room in front of the fireplace, his gaze fell on the chair where she had sat. He sank down in the chair opposite, a wry smile on his lips.

He should have known she was too good to be true. Perfect toned figure. Perfect oval face. Perfect features—arched brows over clear gray eyes with just a hint of blue that reminded him of a calm lake on a summer day. Small nose that twitched intriguingly when she talked. . . . He'd even gone so far as to suspect that the heightened color in her softly curved cheeks was a result of her being drawn to him as he was to her.

Her look of fragility accompanied by a confident manner reminded him of the delicate blossom on the hearty rhododendron bush. Or a ripe raspberry hanging on the vine in late summer. Fortunately, he was not a teenager who might be tempted to reach for the fruit without considering the briars!

He stood and paced the floor again. There was no question about it. She had sparked his interest—her looks, her manner, everything about her. He hadn't been genuinely moved by a woman in. . .how long?

He'd lost count of the number of years that had passed since Kate was killed. She'd meant the world to him, though he couldn't be sure he would have married her. Tragically, she'd gotten mixed up in drugs and the wrong crowd and had been murdered. It was the shock of her death that had changed Elliot's life. And that of his friends. They'd all been forced to grow up overnight. Look at life differently. Take things more seriously. Important things like life, death, and spiritual matters were no longer abstract concepts, but facts with eternal implications.

Even the Briskin issue. When and if he married and had children, Elliot didn't relish the idea of telling them that they couldn't even step into certain sections of Turkey Creek because some of it was on Briskin land.

He hadn't thought about the feud in a long time. Now it was staring him in the face. Maybe he was wrong. Perhaps it was just that any reminder of the Briskins was like someone waving a red flag or like stepping barefoot on one of those excruciatingly painful Chinese chestnut burrs. . . .

He jumped when the phone rang. Joe confirmed his suspicions. The car was registered in the name of a Meera Briskin.

"Thanks, Joe," Elliot murmured. "I owe you one." He wadded up the paper and threw it into the trash can, then stomped toward the door. He stopped, however, with his hand on the doorknob. A wave of nausea churned his stomach and he felt clammy, like he had the flu or something.

It was a disease, that's what it was. The mere mention of the Briskin name was enough to sicken a Maxwell. She'd walked right into his life and infected him with the plague!

Walked right in! Well, no slip of a girl was going to get away with that—particularly not a Briskin. Nausea or no nausea, he'd march out there and order her off his property!

three

In a huff, Elliot wrenched open his office door and stormed into the lobby. "Where'd she go?" he mouthed to Tom, from behind a line of guests the young man was registering.

A light of curiosity glinted in Tom's eyes as he rolled his eyes toward the staircase and grinned.

It was no laughing matter, Elliot thought, but he knew the first thing that would pop into Tom's mind. Well, a romantic relationship with that disturbing young woman was the *last* thing he wanted!

Elliot arrived at the bottom of the stairs just as she reached the third landing. She had a room on the third floor? With his luck, her room would be next to his. Had she planned that too? His blood began to boil.

At that moment she looked down, spotted him, and lifted her hand in greeting. Elliot drew a deep breath. The manager of the lodge couldn't very well shout from the lobby, now could he? He grasped the railing, and the adrenaline rushed through his veins as it had in his football days when he was preparing to make an all-important tackle.

A reprimanding voice stopped him in his tracks. "Mr. Elliot, I told you on the phone I needed you in the kitchen. Where've you been?"

Elliot swiveled around to stare into the worried face of Bertha, the dining room supervisor, who was wringing her pudgy hands. "What is it?" Elliot asked distantly.

"The dishwasher quit."

Trying to focus on the problem at hand, Elliot faced her.

"The dishwasher? Which one?"

"We only have one," Bertha informed him with a sniff.

Elliot lifted his eyebrows. "You should have three. Scheduling is your responsibility. This is a conference check-in day. If you scheduled only one, then I guess you'll have to wash the dishes yourself."

"You got a bug in your breeches, Mr. Elliot?" she snorted. "I'm not talking about no human dishwasher. I'm talking about that mechanical contraption in there. Now, if you want to handle this job. . ."

Elliot knew what he had to do. It wasn't often he scolded Bertha. She was a tough cookie and that's what he needed to keep the dining room running smoothly, especially during summer season when they hired so many young people. But when it came right down to it, the woman had a tender heart.

He put his arm around her plump shoulders and led her toward the dining room, consoling and apologizing. "I'm sorry, Bertha. I'll get maintenance on it right away. In the meantime, I know you can handle things. You're the only one who can at a time like this. . ." He glanced at his watch, "with over three hundred people to feed in less than an hour."

He could trust good old Bertha to get the job done in the kitchen. But it was up to him to handle the likes of Meera Briskin!

❧

By the time he'd gotten maintenance to work on the dishwasher, Elliot's wrath had settled down to a mild case of indignation. The way for a Maxwell to fight a Briskin was not to become infuriated and grab a shotgun, as his own grandfather had, but to keep his cool. At least she probably wouldn't burn the place down while she was staying here.

A Briskin. . .in his lodge! He still couldn't get over it. How and where where had she found the nerve to trespass? But then, she obviously hadn't expected to be caught!

Leaving the kitchen area, he made his way toward the dining room. Many guests enjoyed formal dining from a menu in the Golden Room, but most groups, like this one, found it more convenient and less time-consuming to eat together in the main dining room, where they had a choice of two entrees and several vegetable dishes, along with salad, fruit, and dessert bars.

While the conferees filled their plates from the buffet and seated themselves at the long tables or on the veranda overlooking the mountains, Elliot picked up the microphone and welcomed them. He informed them of the available facilities: a small chapel, an exercise room, swimming pool, and tennis courts. The trails were off-limits to hikers except when accompanied by a guide provided by the lodge. The library shelves were stocked with articles, books, and videos on local history, including the demise of the American chestnut tree and the beginnings of Chestnut Lodge. Amid polite applause, Elliot handed the microphone to Harold Wright, the conference director.

Elliot saw her then, one of the last in line. She looked more like the newspaper picture he had seen, with her flaxen hair framing her face in soft curls. Angel or vixen? He couldn't tell. Only that she looked stunning in a yellow sundress that enhanced her feminine charms. He was acutely conscious that her appeal could easily light a flame in any red-blooded male. That is—if the male didn't know who she was.

Meera Briskin, he said to himself, *I was already a man while you were still playing with dolls, so I just might have a few tricks of my own up my sleeve. What game do you want to play this time?*

She looked his way and his full lips spread into a genuine smile, a smile induced by a fascinating mental picture. It was a picture of Meera the day she fell into Turkey Creek and came up spitting and sputtering, while he stood laughing on the bank, his feet firmly planted on Maxwell property.

～

Meera rushed up the stairs to her room as soon as the "get-acquainted" session ended. She couldn't remember ever having felt so elated. It was as if a whole new world had opened to her, and it had started with her meeting Elliot Maxwell. She was grateful that her first impression had not been colored by her knowing he was a Maxwell, or she might have felt differently.

Part of this euphoria, too, was the motivating keynote speech of Harold Wright, who had inspired her to attempt more than she had ever intended. Then when published writers were asked to stand and tell about their publications, the unpublished had made her feel that she had already accomplished something marvelous.

More importantly, however, was the feeling that she, without the name of Briskin to pave the way, was part of a group who aspired to the same goal: to produce something of value that could be shared with a reading audience.

Even the air seemed charged with electricity. The sheer adventure of all this—being incognito in Maxwell territory—gave her a sense of challenge akin to the reckless danger in which she and Louisa had placed themselves when they'd ridden around the mountain curves on motorcycles as teenagers.

Oh, Clark had presented a sense of intrigue when he'd taken her out into the wilds of Venezuela to his oil fields. But nothing had so elated her as this foray into enemy territory.

Just being near Elliot Maxwell buoyed her spirits. And, of course, she knew why. All of her life she'd been led to believe that a Maxwell was an ogre, ready to murder a Briskin on sight. But tonight at supper, Elliot had told about the lodge's chapel. He'd even mentioned it first in his list of facilities. A family who included a place of worship in their place of business couldn't be all bad.

It was time for all that feuding foolishness to end and the challenge of being the one to end it had created a spark in her that threatened to break out into flame. It was as if a light had been turned on inside herself.

At her door, she flicked on the light in her room. Again she was struck by the room's appearance, as she had been that afternoon. Earlier, the paneled wall, big double bed, and carpeted floor had been awash with golden sunlight flooding into the room from the skylight in the ceiling that sloped down toward her own private balcony. From here, she had a view of the grounds and Olympic-sized pool at the back of the lodge.

Now, with the darkening sky, the light from well-placed lamps lent a warmth to the room, as welcoming as Elliot Maxwell's initial greeting. Suddenly, she wished for a roommate to discuss far into the night this first thrilling session of the conference. Or better yet, she longed for the once close relationship with Louisa, with whom she had shared everything.

That thought brought a slight sinking feeling. Meera wouldn't dare tell anyone, especially Louisa, about this venture of hers. She did need to call home, however.

Laying her notebook on the bedside table, Meera sat on the edge of the the bed, picked up the phone and punched "9," then the number at the Briskin estate. Louisa answered after the second ring.

"Meera! Where are you? Down at Gramps's cab. . .I mean, *your* cabin?"

"Not exactly." Meera couldn't very well tell Louisa, of all people, that she was at Chestnut Lodge on Maxwell property, unless she wanted to be pruned permanently from the family tree.

"What does that mean?" Louisa asked petulantly.

"It means, Cousin, that I wanted to get away for a few days. I have to think."

"The family's starting to worry, Meera. I've called the cabin several times and gotten no answer."

"That's why I phoned, Louisa, so the family won't worry. Please tell them for me that I won't be home tonight."

"Then I'm coming down there. We have to talk."

"No, Louisa!" Meera said quickly. "I told you I'm not at the cabin."

Louisa's exasperation was evident in her loud sigh. "Well, where are you?"

Meera looked down from her third-floor window. A few guests were frolicking in the swimming pool, lighted by the moon and the soft glow of electric lanterns placed high on poles. To the far right of the pool, she spotted Elliot talking with a couple of men she'd seen go into the kitchen earlier.

The men were wearing coveralls and tool-laden leather belts around their waists, so she suspected they were maintenance men. Elliot grasped the arm of one in a friendly gesture, then turned and walked back into the lodge. It was difficult getting used to a Maxwell behaving like an ordinary human being— and a most appealing one at that. But she couldn't admit that to her cousin. "I'd rather not say where I am, Louisa."

Meera heard Louisa's sharp intake of breath, followed by an unmistakable lilt in her voice when she spoke. "Meera! You're with. . .another man."

"I'm not with anyone!" Meera shot back, bristling. "I'm engaged, remember? To Clark!"

At least she had been. Until she'd walked in on Louisa and Clark in each other's arms. No, it wasn't Meera who had forgotten. "I'm. . .spending the night with a friend, Louisa."

"Look, I've got to see you, Meera. We have to talk. I'll be at the cabin first thing in the morning."

"No," Meera said quickly. "I mean, I can't leave in the morning." She had signed up for a class on "Effective Interviews" that she mustn't miss. Not if she was going to do a good job on the Maxwell article—that is, if Elliot allowed her to do it. "Tomorrow afternoon, okay? Say. . .about four o'clock."

"Okay. Tomorrow at four," Louisa conceded. "Be on time, Meera."

"I'll do my best. Now I've really got to run." When Meera hung up, she stared at the phone for a long moment. Talking with Louisa had returned a spark of reality to the situation. A tremulous thought reminded her that she was Meera Briskin, trespassing on Maxwell property, and a shudder traveled down her spine.

"But I'm also Meera Brown," she reminded herself aloud, going into the bathroom and standing by the clawfoot bath-tub as she looked into the mirror and freshened her lipstick. "I'm Meera Brown, freelance writer, on a noble mission, and I will not let Louisa, Clark, or anyone else send me spiraling back into a lifetime sentence of animosity with people I don't even know."

But I want to know them—him! she admitted unashamedly. And with that determination, she switched off the light and headed back downstairs to mingle with other writers in the lovely new world she intended to explore.

❧

It was after nine o'clock before Elliot rolled his sleeves down, put on his suit coat, and left the kitchen. Fortunately, the main-tenance men had managed to get the dishwasher going again and Elliot had made peace with Bertha for the time being. He breathed a sigh of relief when he entered the lobby and heard the murmur and chatter of happy conferees who had finished with their opening session and were now enjoying a reception. Harold Wright, the energetic conference director, strode toward him with a clipboard in his hand and a determined look on his face.

Harold had been bringing the conference to Chestnut Lodge for five years now, liked to work directly with the management, and expected near-perfection. Elliot braced himself for whatever had not measured up to Harold's expectations.

"I'm always a little apprehensive, Elliot," the director began, "as to whether the rooms will be set up properly, the reception ready on time, and everything will be just the way I asked." He shook his head. "Especially this year, since I couldn't work with your dad."

Elliot prepared to offer an apology for some as yet undefined problem. He didn't intend to make any excuses. His dad had had a heart attack three months ago and was now recuperating well, but the doctor had strictly forbade the older man's working for a while. In fact, he was not to put in an appearance at the lodge for quite some time to come. So Elliot had hired a couple of workers to replace himself, but he hadn't seen a need to hire extra management staff. No, this was a challenge that he expected to handle personally—an opportunity to prove something to himself and his dad, he supposed.

Surprised, Elliot listened to Harold's glowing report. "You're doing a great job, Elliot. Everything's running like clockwork: registration, dinner, and as you know, we can't predict what time our "get-acquainted" session will end." He gestured toward the long tables set with refreshments. "But here it is—a fabulous reception waiting for us."

Elliot smiled, not bothering to explain that he had stationed a staff member near the doorway, to let him know when

Harold's session seemed to be winding down. In this business, one couldn't leave anything to chance. "Thanks," he said, breathing a sigh of relief. "Just let me know if there's anything else you need."

Harold reached inside his suitcoat, withdrew a pen from his shirt pocket, and moved the pen along a list on the clipboard. "I do have a few changes."

Elliot grinned. This was more like Harold.

"We'll need an overhead projector in the Laurel Room. Sorry, but the faculty member didn't tell me ahead of time."

"We can handle that."

"And we had more conferees sign up for the 'Inspiration Workshop' than anticipated, so we'll need about five more chairs in Dogwood."

"No problem," Elliot assured him. "Looks like you've picked up in attendance."

Harold nodded. "Trevor Steinbord's coming in as banquet speaker is a real drawing card. I have you to thank for that too."

"How's that?" Elliot asked, registering surprise.

"He said he's a friend of yours and wouldn't want to pass up a chance to come to Chestnut Lodge." Harold's chagrin was obvious. "If I had known that, I'd have asked him a long time ago."

Elliot laughed with him. "I'm looking forward to seeing him again."

Harold glanced around at the happy conferees, buzzing with enthusiasm. "It's such an inspiring place, Elliot. The former students keep coming back, and we've picked up quite a few new ones this year. It's going to be the best conference yet. Enthusiasm's high. Great potential here." His roving gaze fell on one particular student. "Take *that* young woman, for instance. I understand she's going to write an article on Chestnut Lodge."

"You understand. . .what?" Elliot echoed.

Observing the unexpected reaction, Harold added uncomfortably, "During our get-acquainted session she mentioned that you might allow it." He laughed uneasily. "However, beginning writers sometimes confuse aspiration with reality."

Elliot clenched his fists. *The nerve of that woman. First, she trespasses, then she lies, and now she has eliminated any genuine aspiring writer from the competition.* "She did speak to me about it," he conceded, making an effort to recover from that temporary jolt.

"Excuse me," Harold said, gesturing toward a passing faculty member, and away he went.

Elliot hardly noticed. But without really looking, he'd noticed Meera in the crowd. Trying not to appear obvious, he saw how she moved with equal ease among faculty and conferees, relating, fitting in, but in no way blending. Meera Briskin was not one to blend. She was like the angel on top of the Christmas tree—all eyes were drawn to her.

Now she'd gained the conference director's attention. Harold made no bones about this conference being his mission in life. And if Elliot did anything to discourage Harold's "favorite" student, he could wave good-bye to the conference. Now, that would really impress his dad!

No doubt about it, Elliot thought, she was worming her way into his life. . .and into his business, just like the blight that had eaten away at the chestnuts until they were all destroyed. And she was doing it with such ease and grace. But then she'd been reared by experts who had written the book on conniving!

With a mental snort, Elliot grasped a discarded paper cup and threw it into a trash can. More irritating than the label "Briskin" was the packaging. He was a man now, and he knew you couldn't judge a Christmas present by the wrapping anymore than you could judge a book by its cover. This conference provided the apt analogy for that.

If he were honest, however, the scary thing was that if he hadn't found out who she was, he could have been taken in. Totally smitten. Not an easy thing for him. Not with his track record with women.

With determined steps, Elliot strode toward the registration desk. There was one more thing he had to do before the night was over, and that was, without provoking her conference director, to put Meera Briskin in her place.

"Break time already?" Tom asked, looking at a make-believe watch on his wrist when Elliot reached the desk.

Only for a second did Elliot ponder that remark. Tom had no specific break time. His job required his presence for whatever the desk duties demanded, whether registering guests for six hours straight or sitting and doing nothing for the same period of time. Then Elliot remembered that Tom had asked to browse through the display materials at this conference, said he might write a book someday. Seemed everybody said that. He'd even considered it himself. . .briefly. Trevor held the monopoly on celebritydom around here.

"Sure, go on. I'll relieve you for a while," Elliot said to Tom, who quickly left the desk area and began to mingle with conferees at the display tables.

Normally, after being on his feet most of the day, dealing with the innumerable problems of a hotel in keeping his guests pleased, Elliot would be ready to slump into an easy chair or even go to his suite and unwind. Tonight, however, the adrenalin was still flowing. He sat on the high stool that allowed him a bird's-eye view of the lobby, pretending not to be watching for anyone in particular.

He'd tried not to let her get under his skin. Had even tried to convince himself, while standing in a puddle of water in the kitchen, that she was just a conferee who would be here for a few days, then leave. Would that be so terrible?

Perhaps not. But she'd sought him out to ask for an interview. Why? And why not approach him honestly, with a forthright explanation of her intentions? Ha! A Briskin! Honest?

She did have a lot of nerve. The Briskins knew better than to trespass. That was an unwritten law since his grandfather had shot Elias Briskin in the leg, leaving him with a permanent limp. And when his dad had tried to intervene, it had ended up in a fist fight.

Suddenly, unexplainably, Elliot missed Kate. *Kate?* Now what had brought that on? Why was he suddenly aware that he was thirty-two and single?

In that respect, he, Josh, and Trevor were all in the same boat. But Trevor had gone on to achieve fame and fortune as a novelist. And Josh had filled his life with activity—teaching psychology, calling square dances, and working with troubled young people. Elliot, on the other hand, spent most of his time outside office hours simply trying to come to grips with his loneliness. But now it weighed heavily upon his mind. What if? What if Kate hadn't gotten mixed up with drugs? What if they'd married and had kids?

And what if Meera Brown were not a Briskin? Wouldn't that be a most enviable challenge?

Tom returned with an armload of magazines. "Mr. Wright said I could have these," he said with wonder and delight as he placed the reading material under the long bar. He straightened and, keeping his voice low so as not to be overheard, he asked, "Did she have a record?"

"What?" Elliot asked, unable to grasp his meaning.

"You know. . .the license plate." Tom's gaze darted toward the lobby and back to Elliot.

Elliot didn't have long to puzzle over the mischief twinkling in the young man's eyes. For Meera was walking toward him, looking like an angel of light instead of a Briskin with a dark and devious heart. And yes—she definitely had a record. The Briskins represented a long line of pretenders!

She stepped up to the desk, holding two long-stemmed glasses of the lodge's own special nonalcoholic red sparkling punch. She smiled, her soft, shiny lips matching the pink of her fingertips. Her perfume—a fine, delicate scent like yellow jasmine on a balmy spring night—wafted to him from the little pulsepoint on her creamy neck.

"I thought you could use this," she said, offering him a glass.

He accepted it and took a sip, staring into the lying eyes—as clear as a morning sky, as soft as a whisper of mist hovering over a mountain peak. A line from Mary Poppins crossed his mind: "A spoonful of sugar makes the medicine go down," and he swallowed hard over his resolve not to give that sugar-coated beauty the medicine she deserved and kick her out on her ear.

He felt his cheeks flush and was grateful for the cooling liquid. "Thanks," he said and took another swallow. "How's the conference going?"

Meera's face came alive. "Great! For years I've been accused of being a rebel. And tonight in the keynote speech, Mr. Wright used that very word." She set her glass next to his and lifted her fist above her head. "We're not rebels," she said, imitating Harold's enthusiastic manner of speech, "we're pioneers! Communicators! The power of our pens can change the world!"

She laughed and Elliot couldn't help responding to her friendly, congenial manner. "It's my first conference," she confessed.

"What prompted you to attend?" Elliot asked abruptly, wondering if she'd come clean.

Meera decided she would be as honest as possible. "My friend Cathy told me about it. Her brother is the banquet speaker for the conference."

"Trevor Steinbord is a friend of yours?" Was that why Meera had come to the conference? Because of Trevor?

"I doubt that he would call me a friend exactly," Meera admitted and Elliot was inclined to believe her. Trevor was rather a loner like himself and would not use the term lightly. "I suppose *acquaintance* would be more accurate."

Elliot nodded and Meera continued, a little apprehensive now, noting that his manner had changed since their initial meeting. He was such a handsome man, with eyes that could be gorgeous when alight with warmth as they had been earlier. Now he appeared reserved, distant, and his gaze was guarded. What had changed?

"Anyway," she rambled on, "I heard him speak at Chapel Hill. Cathy and I were students there at the same time, and she introduced me to Trevor."

She looked into Elliot's eyes then and something flickered in their blue depths. She felt heat rise to her cheeks. He must think her an idiot to give the impression that an introduction to Trevor Steinbord was the highlight of her life. Good grief, she'd been among the guests at a dinner in Venezuela thrown by the American ambassador!

"I know Trevor," Elliot acknowledged with a cool nod. "His entire family, as a matter of fact. His younger brother was the local football hero before his accident, and his dad designed this lodge."

"I didn't know that." Meera glanced around her, grabbing at this new topic of conversation to ease the awkward moment.

Elliot shrugged. "How could you have known?"

At the edge in his voice, Meera dropped her eyes. He'd already made it quite clear that he usually refused requests for interviews. She was close to tears. It all seemed so hopeless. If she didn't interview him. . .if he didn't get to know her and like her, then her mission would have ended in failure.

No, that wasn't it, she reminded herself. Her mission was not to win the Maxwells' approval, but to discover whether or not she approved of *them*. But somehow, it had become very important that at least one Maxwell—Elliot Maxwell—approve of her.

She lifted her head to look him straight in the eye. "I'm sorry. I've gone about this all wrong."

"You *are* an experienced writer, aren't you?" he asked casually.

"To be honest," she began and Elliot resisted the urge to laugh in her face, "I'm not a creative writer like Trevor, nor do I have any such aspirations. I've only done an occasional factual kind of article, usually a travelogue. The editors liked my writing and gave me an assignment to report on the best inns in western North Carolina."

Once again Elliot clamped his lips shut rather than tell her that all he'd have to do was to pick up the phone and almost any major magazine in the country would send a reporter to cover the story—an experienced one at that. It was almost more than he could do not to reveal that he knew her true identity. But he'd resolved to wait—to see what she was up to. He lifted the glass to his lips and gulped down the contents.

Coolly, with perfect composure, she sipped from her glass, studying him over the rim. Why was she really here, he wondered? If just to attend a conference, then why was she continuing to pursue him—not once, but twice today? He glanced at his glass. It was empty. He'd drained it like a man stranded in the desert. Probably looked like one. Maybe even smelled like one.

"Look," he said, feeling suddenly grungy. "Give me five minutes to shower. Then we'll talk. Okay?"

She nodded. "Don't you ever go home? I mean, don't you have a wife or. . .anything?"

"No wife," he answered abruptly, "or anything." Now why would his marital status concern Meera Briskin if all she wanted was to write an article on Chestnut Lodge? "And I am home," he said, pointing upward, and noticed her surprise. "Third-floor suite."

"You do put in long hours. Are you always so busy?"

Busy? The word struck him as odd. "I suppose," he began, as much to himself as to her, "leisure to me is a walk in the woods, planting a tree. . ."

He paused when he saw her eyes light up with understanding. Then he reminded himself that she was a Briskin. She would know that the Maxwells had been involved in research with the Forestry Service ever since the deadly *cryphonectria parasitica* had destroyed the chestnut. She would know the hard work—cutting, planting, erosion control, ecological studies—these forest lands demanded. The hard work the Maxwells had done through the years just to survive.

But she might not know the damage her presence here could do to his father. "My dad had a heart attack several months ago."

The blue-gray eyes deepened with concern. "How is he now?"

"Doing well. He should be back here before the tourist season begins in mid-June."

Tom looked his way and Elliot motioned to him. "One other thing," he said to Meera as he turned to go. "Before making a decision about your writing the article, I'll need to see your credentials."

He gloated inwardly when he saw the look of chagrin on her face. It felt great to best a Briskin! But what had she expected? Had she actually thought he'd take her at face value, lovely though it was? Now what would she do? 'Fess up. . .or pack her bags and leave?

four

Meera was waiting near the registration desk when Elliot returned wearing a knit shirt and jeans, his still-damp hair curling on his neck. A quick glance told him that she'd exchanged her high heels for flats.

She held out a manila envelope and he felt a tremor vibrating inside. *Get hold of yourself, man!* he scolded himself. He took the package containing her credentials and eyed it as if it were a brown recluse spider. But he wasn't ready to be bitten just yet.

"Put this in my office, will you?" he asked, handing it to Tom.

Seeing the expression of pleasure on Meera's face, Elliot had the distinct impression that the article was not uppermost in her mind, and he determined to find out why. He returned her dazzling smile, but tried to ignore the spark that leapt into her smoky eyes, warning himself that any flame ignited by a Briskin could be as destructive as fire rampaging through the forests during a dry spell.

Feeling warm, he tugged at the collar of his shirt. "Let's walk outside," he said and led her to the back deck that spanned the entire width of the lodge. Guests sat in rocking chairs in casual groupings, admiring the deep purple mountains silhouetted against a violet sky.

"Oh, Elliot," she breathed, "this is. . .beautiful."

He felt certain she'd never seen the distant Briskin mountains from this vantage point. Not only that, she'd probably never spoken to a Maxwell before either.

Deliberately he let his hand touch hers where it lay on the chestnut railing. Her words caught in her throat mid-sentence. But she didn't move away.

Pulling her with him, he led her along the stone pathways and down rustic steps, where they descended the terraced mountainside with its gardens and trees held at bay by stone walls. In the ornamental gardens, Meera found manicured shrubs and fountains playing beneath a grove of giant oaks, maples, and mimosa. Rhododendron sprang up in wild profusion, its showy blossoms almost eclipsing the beauty of the more delicate mountain laurel and fragrant calacanthus.

Elliot's fingers pressed lightly at her waist as he guided her expertly past other guests strolling along the lighted garden paths or sitting on stone benches beneath the tall trees.

When they came to the end of one path, where lush native ferns ran riot, Meera stopped and looked back at the three-story lodge atop the mountain. "I couldn't have imagined all this," she said in a near whisper. "It's. . .magnificent." She turned her glowing face toward his.

Elliot felt his heart lurch. This woman was sincerely moved by the natural beauty surrounding them. *But who wouldn't be?* he decided.

Following a dirt path that led deep into the thick forest, Meera felt a flash of childhood fear—not of bears, rattlesnakes, or mountain lions, but of a dreaded Maxwell lurking behind every tree!

As she walked along beside Elliot, Meera thought how like her own life was this path, dappled with light and shadows. Childhood fears remained, but she was an adult now, coming into the light of her own knowledge. . .about life. . .about the Maxwells.

She liked Elliot Maxwell. She'd liked him on first sight. He had complimented her, had been encouraging, yet had remained polite and respectful. She'd watched him in action, had noted his competence, his concern for his guests, his love for his dad. He was proud of Chestnut Lodge, related well to his staff, was a hard worker. These were attributes she could admire in a man.

As they stepped into the shadows, a nagging doubt surfaced. Where was he taking her. . .and why? He hadn't yet given his permission to write the article, hadn't even looked over her credentials, as far as she knew. This couldn't be part of the coveted interview. So why was he giving her his time?

Still, he was a Maxwell, and she'd always been told that Maxwells were not to be trusted. She wasn't afraid, though, she told herself. One little yell of "Fire!" would echo around the mountainsides, and the sirens would be shrieking to the scene within minutes. Besides, he didn't even know who she was. Could it be that he was as intrigued with her as she was with him?

Meera lifted her hand to her ear. "Do I hear water?"

"Turkey Creek," he explained and gloated at the mental image of her landing kersplat in the middle of it. "On the other side of these boulders."

He reached for her hand and led her along the dirt path, around the rocks, and to the banks of the creek. Directly across from them was the Briskin hunting lodge. "Know what that is?" he asked, watching her closely.

"Well, I—I. . ." she stammered. "It's a cabin. But. . ."

Still hand in hand, Elliot felt the tremor run through her body. He understood why. He'd known it all his life—dread, fear, anger toward the Briskins. She must feel the same about the Maxwells. He pretended not to notice when she attempted to move away, but continued to hold her firm. She had started this. . .she could stay and face the music.

"It's a symbol," he went on relentlessly, ignoring her discomfort. "A mockery. The Briskins built it out of chestnut wood, as a reminder to the Maxwells of their victory in selling us worthless land. It stands there in the clearing like a perennial slap in our faces."

Oh, that's not the reason! she wanted to cry out. What twisted and terrible tales had he been told? But she'd heard the edge in his voice, had seen the hardness in the planes of his face, the bitterness that shimmered in his eyes. She could not dare say what she was thinking: *You're wrong, Elliot! I'm one of them. And my grandfather was one of the kindest, dearest men in the whole world!*

"My dad and granddad brought me here when I was just a kid," Elliot continued, his lips thinned to an angry line. "They took me up and down this creek, pointing out how it ran across Maxwell land in some places and Briskin land in others. But here," he gestured toward the water tumbling noisily over the rocks, "the creek crosses the line in two places. I was warned never to step over that line."

He tossed a look over his shoulder at the boulders and confessed, "I used to hide behind those rocks and spy on the Briskins."

She looked up at him warily. "What did they do to you?" she whispered, as if she didn't know.

"The old man who died last year," he began and saw the flicker of sadness that crossed her face, "sold my granddad thousands of acres of worthless timberland. The trees were primarily American chestnut. . .infested with blight. All of them died. I can show you little shoots that still come up, struggle, then wither away. . .just like the Maxwell fortune," he added bitterly. "The Briskins took it all. For decades my granddad, then my dad fought that blight, but nothing made any difference. It choked off the nutrients while the trees starved to death. It was like watching a loved one suffer, while you stand by, helpless to do anything but watch her die a slow, agonizing death."

Meera felt his pain and sensed that this was not the time to reveal her true identity, or to tell him that he had it all wrong, that her grandfather had not known the trees were blighted. Looking across at the darkened cabin, she felt again her loss. She could almost see her grandfather rocking on the front porch, while she sat on the step looking up at him while he told the Briskin-Maxwell story.

Elias Briskin had discovered ruby in his mountains and had needed money to develop the mines. Jonas Maxwell was eager to buy the land, abounding in chestnut, for his lumber business. The nuts alone would bring a fortune.

In those days, Elias and Jonas were the closest of friends, both competing for the hand of Carrie Spearman, the prettiest girl in the county. But when the blight was discovered, Jonas wouldn't believe that his friend hadn't known in advance. And Carrie, having the highest of standards, refused to speak to him from that day forward and soon announced her engagement to Jonas.

"I would have stepped aside had Jonas won fair and square," Elias often said. "But he poisoned Carrie's mind against me."

It was a dozen years before Elias fell in love again.

"Your grandmother was as sweet and gentle a woman as ever drew breath, yet she'd didn't mind facin' the devil himself if it came down to it. Pretty as a picture, too," he'd told Meera many times. "You put me in mind of her. . . ." Then he'd stare off into the sunset, remembering the young wife who had died when their last child was born.

"I didn't know about the blight," her grandfather always insisted. "Jonas felt I robbed him. But 'twas the other way around. Jonas robbed *me*. . .of my good name, my reputation, my girl, and our friendship."

Then he came to the part that always choked him up. "The day before they married, I tried again. Jonas wouldn't listen to a word I had to say. He chased me down the mountain and, when I got to the creek, I stopped and turned around." Elias would rock, stare at the Maxwell forest, and shake his head as if he still couldn't believe it, even after all those years. "My best friend tried to kill me."

Meera shuddered. Believing that, would Elliot Maxwell listen to her, she wondered, when the time came? For now, she couldn't defend her grandfather, could only ask, "Didn't the trees die on Briskin land too?"

Elliot detected controlled defiance in her tone. "That's not the point," he scoffed. "Their livelihood did not come from the chestnut trees as it did with the Maxwells. With the money they got from selling blighted trees, they developed their ruby mines. I wouldn't be surprised if you're wearing a Briskin ruby yourself." He lifted her hands to take a look.

"Diamonds," she countered as he looked at the dinner ring on the finger of her right hand. "It's my birthstone."

He stared at her hand, narrowing his gaze. The brilliant moonlight that had turned her hair to silver and bathed her face in a soft glow, also revealed a thin white line encircling the ring finger on her left hand. She had worn a ring there recently. Why was she not wearing it now? Was she pretending to be unattached for some reason?

He released her hands and looked at the cabin. "It's been drilled into me that if I ever set foot on Briskin property, I'd be shot on sight."

"Have you?" she wanted to know. "Ever been there, I mean?"

"Never!"

"Then why not now?"

What was she trying to do? Get him shot? "Sure," he

mocked. "I'll just hop over there, and you know what will happen. . . ." He lifted an imaginary rifle to his shoulder and took aim. "*Bang!*"

Meera started at the sound and involuntarily clutched his bicep. "Oh, Elliot," she pleaded, "let's talk about something more pleasant."

Now was the perfect time to set her in the creek—either physically or verbally, or both. In the distance, a wild animal howled and nearby insects hummed to their mates.

He gripped her shoulders. How warm and soft her skin felt beneath his fingers. And benath a velvet sky sprinkled with diamonds, an ingenious plan came to him as naturally as the gentle breeze that stirred her hair. Even the creek seemed to be applauding.

In dealing with the Briskins, his grandfather had used a shotgun, while his dad had used his fists. But then they hadn't been fighting with a beautiful blonde. Surely this generation could come up with something more original.

He looked into her upturned face, her moist lips slightly parted, her misty gray eyes filled with emotion.

There was one way to find out.

With one hand against the small of her back, he entwined the other in her hair, feeling the sensation of corn silk brushing against his palm. Her feathery lashes closed, sweeping her cheeks, as the warmth of her breath mingled with his.

Elliot's lips traced a light pattern over hers, so soft and warm and tasting of sparkling punch. He felt a rush of warmth and pulled her closer. Drawing in an unsteady breath, he covered her mouth with his own in a long, searing kiss.

Suddenly, frightened by her response, Meera wrenched herself away, staring at him with startled eyes. Then she turned from him and hugged her arms to her body, shivering in the cool night air.

Elliot gazed into the distance, watching Maxwell and Briskin water spraying white foam as it churned over rocks in the creek, as if it too were in upheaval, like his emotions. He'd wanted to do that from the moment he'd laid eyes on Meera *Brown*, so he wasn't all that surprised at his own spontaneous action, despite his reservations about Meera *Briskin*.

But he was surprised by the intensity of her response. Or had he imagined that she had grown soft and yielding in his arms? And why had she pulled away? Was it a sudden stab of conscience? Or had she planned this, then been unable to bear the touch of a Maxwell, after all?

Still, suppose she had welcomed it. Now wouldn't her little game be in danger of backfiring?

Somehow he found no satisfaction in that thought. He really didn't wish her any harm. All of his life, he'd simply avoided the Briskins and hoped they'd stay out of his way. But she had crossed the line. That kind of action called for a response. First, though, he'd have to try to discover why she was really here.

"We should be getting back," he said quietly.

"Yes, it's getting late." She ran her fingers through her hair, not quite meeting his eyes.

In a shadowed corner before they reached the patio, he took her hand and felt her tremble. Did she think he would try to kiss her again? But he said what he would have said to any woman whose response to him he might have misinterpreted. "I'm sorry if I offended you."

Offended her? She looked at him wonderingly, overwhelmed that any Maxwell could be such a wonderful human being. He was mistaken about the Briskins, but she'd find a way to remedy that. "Oh, I was not at all offended," she assured him. "I just hope you didn't get the wrong impression of me."

At the moment he had the distinct impression that she wanted him to take her again in his arms, Briskin or not. He lifted her hand and would have brought it to his lips, but remembered the white circle. "Are you. . .married?"

"No." She swiveled out of his reach.

"Engaged?" If she said no, he would ask her about the thin white line.

But she looked at him with unmistakeable misery in her eyes. "I don't know," she whispered into the quiet night. "I really don't know."

Elliot stood like a stone as she hurried away and climbed the steps to the upper deck. She wasn't the only one who was confused. There were several things he didn't know. Why he hadn't thrown her in the creek as he'd planned to do, for instance. And why he'd kissed her instead!

Was he all that cunning. . .or just cowardly? Perhaps his method of dealing with the Briskins was more pleasurable than guns and fists, but it could prove to be catastrophic.

ಶ

Elliot Maxwell's apology echoed in Meera's head all the way to the third floor and even after she had rushed into her darkened bedroom and heard the lock click behind her. For a moment she stood in the shadows, with her back pressed against the door.

She was not offended! She had secretly wanted him to kiss her. Had been fascinated by the idea of finding out if all the Maxwells were of the same stripe. And the feeling had been . . .exhilarating!

Her fingers moved to her lips just as another thought brushed across her mind: Elliot had kissed Meera *Brown*, not Meera *Briskin*. But it had not been Meera Briskin who had kissed him back. That Meera knew better!

No doubt, "Meera Brown" seemed terribly naive or foolish to him. Even when he'd made it clear that he was more interested in her personally than in her writing credentials, she had walked through the dark woods with him and down to the creek. She hadn't even protested when he'd stolen a kiss, had practically asked for it! How could he think she'd been offended?

Suddenly she was aware of light spilling into the room from the skylight and filtering through the windows. Crossing the floor, she stepped to the window and reached out her hand to push back the drape. Her eyes fell on what Elliot Maxwell must have seen—the white band circling her tanned finger. Like. . .a brand. Clearly it was the mark of a ring—Clark's ring—signifying an engagement that she had not acknowledged. An engagement she had considered breaking when he had betrayed her with Louisa.

Clark had almost convinced her that the kiss hadn't really meant anything. Of course, she knew men and women kissed all the time—friendly kisses, innocent kisses, casual kisses. But Elliot's kiss had been anything but casual! And. . .if he learned to like her, maybe that would make acceptance easier when she confessed later that she was a Briskin.

Meera stood at the window, watching while the pool lights were turned out and guests left the area for the night. She replayed her conversation with Elliot, understood his adverse feelings toward the Briskins, hoped someday that their silly family feud would all be behind them. And tried not to give too much credence to the kiss they had exchanged.

At last, Meera opened the glass doors and slipped out onto her private balcony and felt the cool breeze on her flushed cheeks. She scanned the dark mountain peaks silhouetted against the starlit sky and reminded herself that nothing must be allowed to mar that breathtaking view. How many thousands of people must have stood here on Maxwell property, delighting in the natural beauty of the Briskin mountains!

Hearing a splash, she looked down. A lone figure was making swift, graceful strokes through the water. The moonlight glistened on his powerful arms and shoulders while the water sparkled and rippled, accommodating his strong frame.

Meera stared, transfixed, while he swam several laps. Finally he swam to the side, hoisted himself up effortlessly, took a towel from a nearby chair and began rubbing himself dry.

Then he straightened. The moon, as if a spotlight, revealed his well-formed physique—the narrow hips, the tapered waist . . . .

She'd wanted to know what the Maxwells were like. Well, now she knew. At least, she knew that at least one of them was incredibly attractive. It remained to be seen whether there was more to the man than good looks and business savvy.

She returned to the bedroom, still wondering why she had responded to Elliot Maxwell so passionately. Apparently she was drawn to men she should be wary of. Her experience with Clark was teaching her that.

But she didn't want to think of Clark just now. And the thought struck her forcefully: Particularly not Clark!

Later, lying in bed, watching the stars blink above the skylight, Meera thought of how strangely wonderful she had felt in Elliot's strong arms. For those few moments she had even forgotten that he was a Maxwell, her dreaded enemy. She refused to think of the possible consequences if he should discover her identity before discovering that there was more to her than outward appearances.

Shivering, she pulled the covers close around her. Suddenly, the writing of that article took on enormous proportions. It was more than a means to approaching Elliot Maxwell. It was a means of proving herself. And suddenly, she did not feel very confident—only determined.

❧

Elliot had hoped to exercise away in the pool the disturbing memory of his emotional moments with Meera Briskin, to accept the impetuous kiss as a normal reaction to a beautiful, desirable woman, then to leave it behind with the chlorine that was intended to kill germs and prevent disease.

Just then he looked up and saw her stepping from the balcony into the bedroom. And like the bad blood that had existed between the two families for generations, the memory of their brief encounter roiled in his brain. Nothing had been able to eliminate or subdue the blight that had jeopardized his family fortune. Nor had his strenuous swim banished the infestation of Meera Briskin from his mind.

Slipping into his office to change into his clothes rather than meet up with some late-night guest in the hallways or on the elevator, his eyes fell upon the manila envelope on his desk. If he examined it and saw her real name, he'd be obligated to go to her room and demand an explanation. But tonight, feeling his vulnerability, he knew he might be inclined to believe whatever flimsy story she might concoct. Better not risk that.

He dressed quickly and took the elevator to the third floor. His glance swept the hall, stopping on the door of the room where Meera was ensconced. But he entered his own suite, which was in the central part of the building, commanding a view of the Maxwell side of the mountains and the winding road leading to the valley far below.

Showering, Elliot told himself he'd wash all traces of Meera Briskin's elusive fragrance down the drain. Then he dried himself, wrapping a thick towel around his waist. Catching a glimpse of himself in the full-length mirror on the back of the bathroom door, he made a wry face. His emotions had not been in such a turmoil in a long time, but he felt he could explain it. There were two reasons: the Garden of Eden. . .

and Kate.

Just like Adam and Eve, he'd been tempted by forbidden fruit. He'd tasted. And in so doing, his paradise was threatened.

And Kate? She was on his mind tonight, he told himself, because her brother Josh would be at the lodge tomorrow night to call a square dance for the writers' conference.

He switched on the hair dryer and began blow-drying his damp curls. The high-pitched hum of the machine accompanied the poignant thoughts that wouldn't let him be. Seeing the telltale evidence on Meera's finger, he had asked about an engagement. Her words, "I don't know," held the ring of truth. Or maybe he just wanted to believe them. Believe that her intentions were somehow honorable.

He was reminded of the many times he'd asked Kate why she didn't just walk away from her so-called friends who encouraged her drug use. She had cried and said, "I don't know, Elliot. I will. Oh, Elliot, I don't want to live this way. I'll get help, I promise I will!"

And she had tried, really tried. But two weeks after coming out of rehab, she was found dead in a wooded area. She had reportedly OD'd on a lethal drug, and since no conclusive evidence was found to the contrary, her death had been ruled either accidental or a suicide.

Those who knew her best—Elliot, Josh, and the rest of her family—knew she wouldn't have taken her life that way. She would have left a note. Josh had vowed he'd find her murderer someday. Maybe then, they could lay her to rest at last.

Elliot switched off the hair dryer and went into his bedroom to stand in front of the open window, breathing in deep draughts of brisk, fresh air. Far down in the valley, he could see the town's lone traffic light as first one, then another blinked on. Green for go, red for stop. Green for go, red for stop. How symbolic of his own inner chaos.

Turning from the window, he tossed aside his towel and reached for his pajama bottoms. Then he climbed into bed and drew the sheet up over himself.

A stab of loneliness caught him unaware. He hadn't found anyone to fill the void in his life since Kate's death. But he'd accepted it. Oh, there had been a few relationships in the years since she'd been gone, but he'd never kidded himself—or the women—that any of them would lead to a lifelong commitment.

He and Kate had taken for granted that there was something special between them, though they had never made any promises to each other. Then why was she pressing on his mind?

Maybe because he'd learned so much from her misfortune. He and Josh had discussed it many times. Now that Josh was a psychologist, the subject had come up often, along with analysis of many other young people who had not found themselves or gotten a grip on life.

Or maybe he was just looking for some kind of excuse for Meera Briskin having trespassed on Maxwell property and pretending to be someone she was not. Kate had come from a basically moral family, with high standards. If someone like that could go astray, then what chance did a Briskin have?

He reached over to the bedside table and switched on the radio, hoping to distract himself from this litany of conflicting thoughts. Much later, somewhere in the oblivion of another world, he heard the sound of a crooner singing a plaintive love song from a bygone era: "I try hard. . .not to give in. But I've got you. . .under my skin."

Perfume filled the air. . . . Corn silk cascaded through his fingers. . . . A longing took possession of him, and he awakened with a thudding heart, murmuring the words the crooner had sung.

His eyes flew open and he stared into the night. It was not Kate who had invaded his senses. It was *Meera*.

A terrifying realization penetrated his consciousness. Meera Briskin had not disappeared with the night. She was not, after all, something he could scrub off his skin. She was real and warm and alive. . .and she was driving him to distraction.

five

Early morning was Meera's favorite time of day, but she couldn't ever remember a dawn as gorgeous as this one. She rubbed her eyes and peered again through her bedroom window at Chestnut Lodge. The low clouds, hugging the mountaintops as if in a last farewell, slowly lifted, revealing the scenery an inch at a time, as if God were completing a mountain landscape on the canvas of the sky.

She could barely keep her mind on the devotional reading for the day. But she had no problem whatsoever in her morning prayer time, keeping her eyes open and praising God for the beauty of the early sun touching the mountainsides that she had explored, roamed, hiked through, but had never before viewed from this angle.

Delicate white dogwood blossoms, keeping their promise of spring, were bringing to life a forest that had lain dormant all winter. Tender new leaves sprouted from the limbs of trees. And though she couldn't see them from here, she knew that wild flowers, bulbs, ferns, and myriads of other colorful blossoms were springing up all over the forest floor. The air was fragrant with the scent of new life.

Meera knew in her heart that, if her family insisted upon selling the mountain, it must be offered to the Maxwells first. To take this view from Elliot or to mar it in any way would surely be a terrible injustice.

Her gaze wandered down to the pool. Its smooth surface reflected the first light in a shimmering haze. But in her mind she saw Elliot, and she looked for him, half expecting to see him farther down the mountain, toward the creek, near the outcropping of rocks where he'd held her in his arms.

Meera shook off the heady memory. She reminded herself sternly that she was no longer paying attention to her prayers. Or was she? Wasn't it her heart's desire that somehow this ridiculous animosity between the Briskins and the Maxwells would end?

Like spring, this was a new generation, a new era. She liked Elliot Maxwell. And he liked her—even if he did think the woman who had caught his fancy was Meera Brown. This was a time for new beginnings. She must tell him who she was and why she was here. He would understand. And it would be foolish to wait until she'd written an article. That was such a small thing compared to two people healing old hurts and building a better relationship, rather than letting them lie, rotting like fallen logs on the forest floor.

"I'll tell him who I am," she whispered aloud. "The very first chance I get. I'm sure he'll appreciate what I'm trying to do. I just know it."

On that resolve, she quickly showered, shampooed, dried her hair and twisted it into a topknot, pulling a few short strands over her brow. There were more important things to do than worry about her appearance, so she applied mascara only and a light lipstick after slipping into a blue sundress and sandals.

She would begin by asking Elliot if he'd looked over her credentials and read her articles. She didn't even want to imagine that he might turn her down. Not after last night. No, she'd keep a positive attitude.

But she didn't see him at breakfast. She sat next to Marlene, another Southerner she'd met at the "get-acquainted" session. The animated conversation at the table kept her spirits buoyed, and Meera felt again the same surge of hope she had felt during the keynote speech the night before, when Harold Wright had so motivated her, making her believe she could accomplish much with her writing if she simply gave it the attention it deserved.

For the next few hours Meera attended several workshops, including "Effective Interviews," and found the information to be invaluable if she decided to pursue a writing career.

The session on "Inspirational Writing" did just that for her. It seemed incredible but she began to believe that her words might inspire others as she had been inspired during the morning. Why, with all the insights she was sure to glean during her experiment at Chestnut Lodge, she'd have enough material to write a book on resolving family squabbles! Somehow, though, the family squabble no longer loomed as large as it had all her life.

Elliot just had to understand. Her eagerness to talk with him began to wane slightly when she didn't see him during the morning break. Neither he nor Tom were at the registration desk. A different clerk was on duty, and a mature woman appeared to be in charge. Nor was Elliot anywhere to be seen at lunchtime either.

After lunch, Marlene and some others had planned to go into Asheville. But Meera turned down the invitation to join them. Instead, she bought a few books in the conference bookstore and browsed through the display tables in the lobby.

But her mind was not on effective writing techniques or how to conduct a successful interview. *Maybe he read the articles and didn't like them,* she fretted. Maybe her credentials weren't professional enough. Or. . .maybe he was regretting the kiss and was having trouble facing her.

Worse yet, maybe he had learned her true identity—the scenario played itself out in her mind—and his dad had had a relapse. . . . It was a terrifying thought to imagine that she might be the cause—however unintentionally—of even more problems for the Maxwells. If so, there would never be a chance to end the hard feelings between the two families!

By mid-afternoon Meera was ready to leave the lodge for her appointment with Louisa. She was almost tempted to keep driving and never look back. Maybe this was a harebrained idea in the first place.

As she sped along the Parkway, taking the scenic route, the panoramic views that spread out before her around every turn lifted her spirits. How could she have succumbed to such doubt and worry when the One who had created all this also had the answer to her problems? Of course! Elliot Maxwell simply had a day off. And there was no reason why he should have reported to her. Smiling at her foolishness, she switched on the radio and listened to inspirational music as she drove through the mountains and onto Briskin property.

Louisa's black sports car, with Louisa still at the wheel, was parked in front of the cabin when Meera drove up. She pulled around back—just in case Elliot Maxwell might be strolling through the woods or down by the creek.

Louisa bounced out of her car and walked around to meet Meera, her dark eyes flashing. "What took you so long? You know I don't like being out here in the boondocks alone!"

Meera stepped up onto the porch and opened the back door. "Sorry. I got away as soon as I could."

"You know, anybody could be hiding in there," Louisa remarked skeptically, standing back until Meera had checked it out.

"Grandfather Elias always said that's partly what the cabin's for. Sometimes people get lost in the forest. They're welcome to find shelter here."

"Humph! Sounds dangerous to me," Louisa sniffed. "Besides, you can't trust anybody these days. They'll take advantage of you."

Meera didn't reply to that. Her own cousin—her lifelong friend—had taken advantage of any opportunity to flirt with Clark. . .until he finally responded.

"There's no coffee," she said, holding up a box of teabags. "But I'll heat some water for tea." While the water heated, she took inventory of the cupboards, mumbling, "Have to buy groceries soon."

Louisa lifted a sable brow. "Then what *have* you been doing all this time, Meera?"

Meera looked over her shoulder. "Let's just say it's something I've wanted to do for a long time."

Louisa's mouth flew open and her eyes widened. "You've been hang gliding!" she said and plopped down in a kitchen chair.

At that ridiculous observation, Meera laughed and turned to face her cousin, not bothering to correct the impression. "Well. . .it's challenging, dangerous, and quite intriguing," she replied, describing how she felt about the Maxwell venture.

"Why didn't you ask *me*?" Louisa pouted.

"That's something people should decide for themselves, Louisa. Now what's so urgent that you had to see me today?"

Her cousin rose, still eying Meera quizzically. "We need to know if you're going back to Venezuela with us next week. We have to make arrangements, you know."

"I'm not going yet." Meera reached inside a cabinet for two cups and saucers. "I have a lot of thinking to do and I can't do it in Venezuela."

"You're not wearing Clark's ring," Louisa said with surprise, noticing the bare finger. "What does that mean?"

"What does it mean?" Meera said, and the cups rattled against the saucers as she set them on the cupboard. "Really,

Louisa, do you expect me to wear a rock like that while hang gliding?"

"You're not hang gliding now."

"No, and the ring is in a safe place." Meera got up and walked to the window, remembering the day she had walked in on Louisa and Clark in the midst of a passionate embrace. Seeing her, they had quickly sprung apart, looking sheepish. Later, Clark had tried to insist that it had been only a friendly hug. Then he'd put Meera on the defensive, accusing her of keeping him dangling. He didn't want to wait any longer.

But how could Clark, if he were serious about marrying her, have embraced Louisa so passionately? For that matter—and she blushed to think about it—how could she herself, if she was serious about Clark, have responded so ardently to Elliot Maxwell?

Maybe it was because she had been so overwhelmed to find a decent Maxwell that she had felt like celebrating! At least, she wouldn't have to teach her children to hate the Maxwells—to distrust them—to carry bitterness in their hearts all of their lives. No, it wasn't the same as the incident between Clark and Louisa at all, Meera told herself. She had not been responding to a man, but to a miracle.

How different Elliot and Clark were, she thought, staring at the teabags steeping in identical cups. Elliot was more serious than Clark, but he was six or seven years older, a mature man with heavy responsibilities. Having done some ecological studies herself, she had to be impressed with the Maxwells' work in that area, including forestry, and expected that Elliot, too, was personally involved. She admired his ability to run the resort, serving his guests efficiently while keeping the surrounding forests well maintained.

Clark would be entering the last year of his doctoral program in the fall, but he was primarily interested in spending his allowance. She smiled. That was not a complaint. She'd helped him spend it on more than one occasion! They'd had some exciting times together.

But this—this feeling for Elliot Maxwell—was something entirely different. There had been that wonderful moment when she'd lost all sense of who she was and why she was trespassing on Maxwell property.

"Twenty-five thousand dollars for your thoughts," a voice said in one ear while the teakettle whistled in the other. "Meera," Louisa said sharply, "are you listening to me?"

"I'm sorry." Meera reached for the whistling kettle. "I didn't hear you."

"I asked," Louisa said, looking at her strangely, "what will Clark think about your not coming back with us?"

"Why don't you ask him, Louisa?" Meera retorted, quite certain that her cousin needed no encouragement to do just that.

"You're still upset about the day you walked in on me and Clark, aren't you?"

Meera sighed and brought the cups to the table. "Yes and no, Louisa. If you and Clark are interested in each other, then I won't stand in your way."

Louisa snorted. "Meera, you know good and well that any guy who gets a good look at you and your blond hair never gives me a second glance!"

"That's not exactly a compliment, Louisa."

"I didn't mean it as one," her cousin replied saucily. "It's just the truth."

Meera felt a sudden wave of nostalgia. She'd grown up with this girl. Louisa had been an only child, getting everything she'd ever wanted. . .except time with other children and a family life where one learned the art of sparring and sharing. Louisa had never learned to share. She'd always wanted whatever Meera had—including her current love interest.

"Was that all you wanted to talk to me about, Louisa?"

The dark-haired girl poked at her teabag with a spoon. "I wanted to explain, Meera. I was going to when we were in Venezuela—then we got the word about Gramps and. . ."

Grandfather Elias, as Meera had called him, had been her closest friend. Under his tutelage, she had learned to care about the forests, the mountains, and the Creator who had carved them out of the wilderness. She wanted to spend time at the cabin alone, remembering and cherishing the memory of their times together.

"Don't worry about it, Louisa," Meera consoled, her heart going out to the girl who often seemed so lost. Louisa had everything, yet was unsure of herself. "We'll just say it was a mistake and I forgive you."

Louisa's eyes widened. "Oh, but it wasn't."

"What?"

"I mean," Louisa hastened to explain, "I. . .like Clark. It would be a mistake for you two to marry if he didn't even know I was in the running until it was too late."

"Oh, Louisa, you haven't changed a bit!" Meera sighed. "You've always made a play for any man I was ever interested in."

"I just wanted to see if I could take them away from you," Louisa admitted smugly, then on a serious note, "but this is different. That day with Clark, I just couldn't help myself.".

Before last night Meera could easily have replied that there was no excuse for them to have been in each other's arms. It was betrayal of trust, blood relationship, and friendship. At the moment, however, she had no room to talk.

Louisa filled the awkward silence. "Meera, do you really want to marry a man who can't stay away from me?"

Meera's stormy eyes met Louisa's. "So that wasn't the only time!"

"Yes. . .it was," her cousin admitted, and Meera believed her. Judging from her downcast appearance, she was telling the truth. "But once is enough, isn't it? I mean, it sure sent you into a spin."

"I felt betrayed. . .by two people who are supposed to be close to me. But like I said, I'm willing to forgive."

"Well, that's certainly a change of heart."

Meera drew herself up. "I think it's possible for a man to be tempted by a woman, and his response doesn't necessarily mean he's fallen for her. It may not have anything to do with love at all."

Louisa eyed her skeptically. "You don't talk like yourself, Meera."

"Maybe I'm growing up, Louisa. And it's time you did too."

"I've grown up enough to know I'll fight for what I want, Meera," she threatened.

Meera stared at her. "There's no contest, Louisa. I'm engaged to Clark. He asked me to marry him, and nothing has changed. . .even after that unpleasant little episode you concocted."

"I didn't find it unpleasant," she said spitefully. "And neither did Clark."

"Remember what I said about temptation." Meera toyed with her cup.

"Then you're going to stay here while I return to Venezuela?"

"Well, I don't intend to ride herd on you or Clark or anybody else for the rest of my life."

"You're that sure of yourself, huh?"

Meera didn't feel sure at all. She had grown less sure of her feelings for Clark over the past year—and in so doing, she'd grown less sure of herself. To reject Clark would seem like the ultimate rebellion—in defiance of what appeared to be a perfect match, a union that would greatly please both families. She didn't know the answers. And it seemed that each day she further complicated her own life. "Look, I've got to go, Louisa. I have an appointment."

Louisa nodded and got to her feet. "Let me leave first. I don't want to be stranded down here on the road somewhere. There might be a Maxwell on the prowl."

Meera watched her cousin drive away, thinking how often she had made similar comments about the Maxwell family. But she was tired of perpetuating that silly prejudice—not without evidence. And so far, the evidence she'd seen exhibited by Elliot Maxwell was nothing to fight about.

She pulled away from the cabin after Louisa's car was out of sight. She'd gone too far to back out now, and she found herself actually looking forward to returning to Chestnut Lodge, where she would revert to being Meera Brown, freelance writer.

Engrossed in her thoughts, Meera failed to notice the lowslung black sports car parked behind a grove of trees. Nor did she see it follow her as she pulled out onto the highway, keeping well back but never losing her.

≈

While the day manager was on duty at the lodge, Elliot visited his dad and mom. He'd jogged down the exit and taken the private road from there, hiking out to the family home a couple of miles beyond.

The house was a contemporary marvel—completely round, built of stone, cedar, and glass, and perched on the side of the mountain with a breathtaking view of the lower mountains and valleys stretching as far as the eye could see.

It's all God's, he thought. *It doesn't belong exclusively to*

either the Briskins or the Maxwells, and we sure can't take
it with us. True, he argued with himself, *but we've got to get*
along with each other on this earth. God put us here to live
together in harmony and to have dominion over the earth.
Sure, there was such a thing as forgiveness, but there was
also such a thing as taking a stand on what's right and wrong.
Even though Meera had had nothing to do with the terrible
injustice that had triggered the feud, she belonged to the
Briskin family. And regardless of his personal feelings, there
was a family loyalty to which he must adhere.

A warmth, different from that of the sun beating down upon
him, welled up within when he saw his dad on his knees,
working in a flower bed.

"Morning, Dad," Elliot greeted his father as the older man
walked up, wiping beads of perspiration from his forehead.
"How's it going?"

"Great, son." His dad's laughter held a touch of irony. "I,
who have cut trees and lifted logs all my life, am now re-
duced to *this*!" He flourished a handful of crabgrass, then got
to his feet and stripped off his gloves.

Seeing the scowl on Elliot's face, he put his arm around his
son's shoulders. "Oh, I'm not complaining. In fact, I feel a
little guilty because I'm enjoying this so much. It even occurs
to me—and Janie likes the idea—that I might just retire from
the lodge. Oh, I could do some bookwork or something, but
I've been needing to slow down. Now come up here and tell
me how things are falling apart over there without me."

Elliot laughed this time. Strange how, as he'd grown older,
he'd come to appreciate his dad's sense of humor. It seemed
that the heart attack had only reaffirmed the depth of his love
and respect for his father. He had to face the fact that he would
lose him someday—maybe sooner than he wished—and it
was not an easy thought.

His dad sat in the swing and Elliot dropped down beside him. From the smile on the older man's face, Elliot knew he was pleased with his progress report. It's what his dad had always wanted—a son to follow in his footsteps.

That subject exhausted, his dad began to reminisce, retelling stories of Elliot's childhood, never mentioning the Briskins, as if they had dropped from the face of the earth. Elliot was quiet, recalling how his father had often told Bible stories as well, including the one about the Garden of Eden. "As you grow up, Elliot," he'd said seriously, "you'll be tempted to eat of the fruit of forbidden trees. . .just like Adam and Eve. That fruit comes in many forms. But if you eat of it, you'll have to pay the consequences."

His dad hadn't mentioned that story in years. No doubt he expected Elliot to have learned that lesson by now.

While Elliot had filled his dad in on most of the latest news, he had carefully avoided mentioning the proposed article. No way could an article about the Maxwells be written by a Briskin. It would kill his dad.

"You look worn out, Elliot," his mom said over their lunch of beef stew and hard rolls. "Max, this boy's working too hard."

"Now, Mother, he knows he can hire all the help he needs. Besides, a little hard work never hurt anybody."

Elliot shrugged. "It's not the work. I just didn't get much sleep last night."

Jane Maxwell looked over the rim of her tea glass, then set it down with a little thud. "You've got a girl, Elliot," she said hopefully.

"No," he denied, and hurriedly took a bite of stew as a defense against further conversation.

When he glanced up, he saw the gleam in his mom's eyes. It was no secret that she was eager for her only son to find somebody, settle down, and give her some grandchildren and Maxwell heirs.

He shook his head again, but the light in her eyes remained.

"Well, it's nothing to be ashamed of, is it?" she persisted. "After all, it's about time."

"Don't start that again," Max said to his wife.

Jane insisted that Elliot take a nap, and he lay across the bed in his old room. He had moved into Chestnut Lodge when he'd begun working there while attending college. But occasionally, it felt good to come home and let his mom treat him like a little boy again.

It was late afternoon when he returned to the lodge and learned from the manager that all was well. Bertha had the dining room under control, Tom was manning the desk, and no complaints had been registered with the conference director. Satisfied that all the guests were being well cared for, Elliot stepped into his office to catch up on some paperwork and to make decisions about applications from college students wanting summer jobs.

He had not been at his desk long when a knock sounded on the door. At his invitation, big Joshua Logan came in, looking like a burning bush with his heavy beard and mustache and an unruly thicket of auburn curls springing up all over his head. Kate's hair had been that color. But she'd been a good foot shorter than her brother, who stood several inches over six feet.

At the moment, Dr. Josh Logan resembled anything but a psychology professor in his square-dance costume—Western jeans, cowboy boots, and a white pleated shirt with a red bandana knotted at the neck.

"Josh!" Elliot hurried around the desk and put out his hand. "Good to see you, buddy. Where have you been keeping yourself this last month?"

The two settled into the lounge chairs in front of the fireplace and caught up on their activities. It was good having Josh back in town. For the past eight years, he'd been teaching in Charleston. Now he was back to fill an opening at the University of North Carolina at Asheville. Josh had told Elliot that those years away had given him time to cool off after his sister's murder, and he could now go about the business of finding the murderer more objectively. Elliot knew Josh's mind would never be at rest until that case was solved.

"School was out last week, so all that's behind me till fall," Josh said with some relief. "What's new with you?"

Elliot shook his head. "I'm really not sure." He picked up the unopened manila envelope on his desk and handed it to Josh. "Take a look at this."

Josh removed the papers, examined them casually, then glanced over at Elliot. "Nice-looking magazines, El. Am I supposed to be looking for something in particular?"

"The author, Josh. Look at the name on the paper-clipped articles."

"Meera Brown," Josh read. "So?"

"Let me see that!" Elliot reached for the magazines. He'd been so sure she had written under her real name that he hadn't bothered to look. "So, I've been duped again," he said ironically and explained his dilemma. "She's a *Briskin*, Josh."

Josh was puzzled. "But what has she done to you, pal? Or is this a carry-over from three generations back?"

Elliot sighed heavily and leaned his head against the back of the chair. "Oh, I have no personal grudge. But I've always accepted the fact that as a Maxwell, I'd be loyal to the family. As far as I know, they haven't done anything to *me* . . . until now, that is. Now she comes along, pretending to be this Meera Brown."

Josh tapped on the magazine, pointing to the byline.

"A pseudonym," Elliot explained. "She's still a Briskin."

"But she's also Meera Brown, writer, attending a writer's conference."

Elliot understood what Josh was getting at. His sister Kate had been two different people too. One was the moral, intelligent, attractive young woman from a good middle-class family. The other was a person addicted to mind-altering drugs. The real Kate had been buried deep inside somewhere, and all her friends and family had tried in vain to reach her.

He and Josh had talked it over many times—how they'd become more tolerant of troubled people, less judgmental, since the experience with Kate. "But this is different, Josh," Elliot insisted. "We knew Kate's behavior was drug-induced—although I'm not excusing that. But Meera's is deliberate."

"Would it be so bad to let her write the article under the name of Brown?"

Elliot let out a sigh of exasperation and rose to pace in front of the fireplace. "Josh, it's not just the article. The woman seems to be going out of her way to get to me."

"And apparently she's succeeded."

Pausing in front of his friend, Elliot stared. "For the first time in many years, I've let my guard down. That is, I could be vulnerable if I didn't know who she really was."

Josh pulled on his beard thoughtfully. "Do you? Know who she really is, I mean?"

The implication was obvious. The drugged Kate was not the real Kate. Not at all.

Elliot shoved his hands in his pockets and continued pacing. "That's the problem. I don't really know. I know she's a Briskin. But then, there's this beautiful, warm, very appealing woman I'd like to know better." He shook his head sorrowfully.

Josh nodded. "I understand where you're coming from, Elliot. But as any good psychologist will tell you. . ."

"I can't tell you what to do," they finished in unison.

Josh laughed and stacked the magazines neatly. "But I will say this: If fueling your family's feud is your objective, then order her to get off your property."

He grinned at the doleful look on Elliot's face. "On the other hand, if you're serious about getting to know her as an individual, then perhaps you might ask not what she might be doing to you, but what you can do for her. There's a tremendous opportunity here, Elliot."

"I know you're talking in spiritual terms, Josh," Elliot said hesitantly.

"Yes, and I know you're thinking physical. I understand. I'm an old single guy myself, remember? And we are physical beings, as well as spiritual."

Elliot smiled wryly. "I guess what it comes down to, Josh, is what I've known all along. Which Meera do I want to deal with? And more importantly, in what manner?"

six

Meera arrived at the lodge before suppertime, quickly showered and changed, then stopped by the desk to ask Tom if Elliot had left anything for her.

"Sorry," Tom replied, "nothing."

She walked across the lobby, trying not to feel rejected. After all, she'd learned in the writing classes that it takes longer for an editor to say yes than it does to say no. The same principle could apply to an interviewee, she consoled herself. Or maybe he wanted to give her his reply in person. Her heart skipped a beat, both in fear and in anticipation.

Brushing aside these conflicting emotions, Meera gratefully acknowledged the approach of Marlene, who was decked out in a wide-brimmed straw hat, coveralls, red shirt, and a red and black bandana.

Marlene waved and hurried over. "You look great, Meera, but then you always do."

"I wasn't sure what to wear," Meera admitted. "The brochure said 'Western square dance.'" She glanced down at her full skirt of stonewashed denim paired with a ruffled peasant blouse. Her hair, falling in one long braid over her shoulder, was tied with a ribbon. "I think my costume may be more 'Spanish' than 'Western.'"

"I think mine's more 'hillbilly,'" Marlene said, wrinkling her nose in dismay and thrusting her hands into the pockets of her coveralls.

Meera laughed at her new friend's rueful expression. "Look over there." Several of the women were dressed in skirts styled with tiers of ruffles over stiff crinoline petticoats.

Marlene shrugged. "Well, it looks like anything goes. Let's head into the dining room."

The table decor—red and white checkered cloths and bright red napkins—carried out the Western theme. A tape playing country-western music set the mood of the evening.

Glancing around, Meera saw that Elliot was again nowhere in sight and tried not to be disappointed. She tried telling herself that if she never saw him again, she had already gained much with the week's discoveries and should be counting her blessings.

"Mmm," she said, taking her own advice. "This barbequed chicken is delicious."

"And wait till you taste the baked beans! Heavenly," Marlene sighed, closing her eyes in ecstasy. "Must be an authentic recipe."

After supper the group moved to the tennis courts, located beyond the steps at the back of the lodge, where Meera and Elliot had walked the night before.

There she spotted Elliot who was scurrying around, checking cables hooked up to some sound equipment on a table. He, too, was wearing jeans and a Western-style shirt with a braided leather tie. In his boots, he appeared even taller and more striking than ever.

Then her attention turned to the big bearded man who was testing the microphone. "One—two—three. Josh Logan here. Good evening, pardners." Meera and Marlene exchanged dubious glances, having already discussed their ineptness at square dancing.

But soon she was caught up in the exhibition of colorfully costumed professionals who stomped and turned and twirled as their appreciative audience looked on, applauding wildly. At the conclusion of the performance, Joshua told them that the experienced dancers would now mingle with the crowd, dancing with the inexperienced ones, and the costumed group headed for the sidelines. Meera thought one man was staring directly at her, when suddenly he held out his hand and asked Marlene to dance.

Feeling a little embarrassed, she was wondering why she had been passed up when she sensed someone standing behind her. His warm breath tickled her ear as a deep voice asked, "May I have this dance?"

She turned and looked up into Elliot's smiling blue eyes. There was no guardedness in his expression, only pleasure in seeing her again, it seemed. In fact, his lingering look set her pulses to racing. So she was being completely honest when she replied regretfully, "I'm afraid I don't know how."

He surprised her by saying, "It would spoil the fun if you did. Come on. I'll give you your first lesson."

Meera gave him a scrutinizing look. "Have I shrunk, or are you wearing high heels?"

His lips twitched slightly. "That's a dangerous kind of statement," he warned.

"I live dangerously," she said with a flippant toss of her head, and pushed away the truth of her statement. What would he do if he knew a Briskin was deliberately flirting with a Maxwell?

She placed her hand in his outstretched one and they walked out onto the tennis court. She was strongly tempted to tell him the truth about her charade. Was this the right time? Would he take her in his arms and assure her that it didn't make any difference?

"The answer is yes," he said abruptly.

Meera inhaled sharply. Had she actually voiced her thoughts? "Did. . .I ask you a question?"

He nodded. "Several times, in fact. I believe you wanted to

write an article, didn't you?"

Her eyes lit up with relief and understanding. "Oh, so you're granting me permission?"

At a second nod from Elliot, Meera's heart thudded. Maybe . . .just maybe her mission would be accomplished after all.

"Thank you," she whispered just as Josh called, "Make a big circle. Ladies on the men's right. Now all join hands and circle left."

She followed Elliot's expert lead, circling left, then right, then allemanding with her corner, taking the arm of the person on her right and swinging around, then returning to her partner. *Partners!* A Briskin and a Maxwell! Only in this moment of fantasy would such a thing be possible, she decided.

There was no time to think beyond that, for Josh called out, "Now dosey-do!" and she and Elliot circled each other back to back, then obliged when he added, "Now look your partner in the eye." Her eyes met Elliot's laughing ones.

"I must look ridiculous," she said, breathless, aware of Elliot's easy rhythm and grace.

"Au contraire. . . ." He swung her close before twirling her around and taking both her hands in his. "It gets easier with practice."

With time, she thought. What would time bring? Was there any hope that the animosities between the Maxwells and Briskins could ever end? Or was she just a fool—rushing in where angels feared to tread?

❧

Meera and Elliot stood in line for ice cream, then found seats in folding chairs set up around the tennis courts to watch another exhibition by the professional dancers he had hired for the evening.

"Do you do this often?" Meera wanted to know.

He finished a big bite of strawberry ice cream, then smiled. "Not very often. But I used to dance a lot. . .in my younger days."

"Your younger days?" Meera would have laughed, but his face had taken on a serious expression and there was a distant look in his eyes.

He glanced at her. "Josh, the caller, is the brother of a girl I was very close to. Since her death, I suppose I haven't considered myself very young anymore."

"You could have fooled me out there," Meera said quietly.

"I even fooled myself." He looked her directly in the eye. "Since Kate's death, my social life has been somewhat curbed."

He said it matter-of-factly, but Meera could see the stiffening of his jaw. His ice cream was melting, and she set her own half-eaten bowl next to his.

"Do you have any more classes tonight?" Elliot asked at last, breaking the long silence.

"No."

"Then let's walk. . .and talk about. . .the article."

"Yes," she agreed in a small voice.

They disposed of their plastic dishes, and Elliot glanced at Josh who was ready to call another dance for the conferees. Josh winked, but his expression was sober, acknowledging his concern for his buddy. No woman who followed his sister Kate in Elliot's affections would have an easy time of it. . . particularly if her name was Briskin.

As they walked, the music faded and the sun's last rays flamed in the sky, painting the horizon with gold and orange. As if in homage to the dying day, the insects began to make their own music.

"You were in love with Kate?" Meera asked.

"I don't know," he admitted. "I suppose that's why I could

identify with you when you said you didn't know whether you were engaged or not. If things had been different, Kate and I might have made a lifetime commitment. In any event, no one else has come along who has meant as much to me as she did." He shrugged. "Maybe it was love. . .or maybe it's just that I hate to see a promising life wasted."

"She. . .died, you said?"

"Several years ago. It was on TV, in the papers. You may have read about it. It happened on a hot day in mid-July."

Meera shook her head. "No. But several years ago I was spending my summers abroad." There was a long pause, then she added softly, "You can't forget her, can you?"

He gazed out at the distant mountains. "I've never found a woman who could make me forget. . ." Hesitating, he turned to face her, grasping her shoulders with both hands, "Until you, Meera, until you."

Meera held her breath, then swallowed hard. "Then I'm. . . therapeutic."

"Hardly," he moaned. "You're more disturbing than any woman I've ever met, Meera. . .Brown!"

So that was it! he explained to himself. When she was in his arms, she was not a Briskin—she was sweet, lovely Meera Brown, freelance writer. Or maybe she was just playing the part to the hilt. If so, just how far would she go with this act? And a more pressing question still—how far would *he* go?

Then he recalled that Briskins were masters at pretense. There had been many years of friendship between their grandparents, so Elias Briskin had apparently faked that too. And his blood ran in Meera's veins.

Elliot knew she was pretending to be Meera Brown, and in that role he'd sensed a certain innocence in her warm, passionate kisses. But Meera Briskin was a confident, rich socialite from a dubious background, who could buy whatever she wanted, go anywhere, do anything. And that Meera wore the impression of a band on the ring finger of her left hand.

He closed his eyes to clear his head. Josh had made him see, without really saying it, that he had a responsibility not just to react to Meera—but to be the kind of man she needed him to be, the kind of man he should be. But it wasn't easy when his heart were saying one thing and his mind another.

He opened his eyes and reached for her hand. The heightened color in her cheeks betrayed her excitement—or what he interpreted as excitement. She even managed to look disappointed when Elliot stepped away to lead her from the terrace to a more secluded area.

The truth was, Meera had mixed emotions. She had half-hoped he would try to kiss her again, but all her instincts told her it was wrong to continue to mislead him. She must tell him. . . *now*. He would have every right to resent her if she allowed him to care for her while she deliberately concealed her identity from him. "Let's walk down to the creek, Elliot," she said, making the decision at last.

Elliot felt a sudden elation. Perhaps she was ready to open up. Or maybe she was just bored with her life and had decided to play cat and mouse with a Maxwell. Even so. . .even so. . .he still had an obligation as a mature man dealing with a possibly errant young woman.

When Meera heard the babble of the creek, an old melody ran through her head: "Love and marriage, love and marriage, go together like a horse and carriage. . . ." Years ago, she and Louisa had chanted: "Briskin and Maxwell, Briskin and Maxwell, go together like skin and poison ivy."

At least, if her confession caused him to break out in red splotches, she could escape to the other side of the creek. Surely a Maxwell would never follow her there!

When they reached the boulders, they climbed up to sit and

look down on the murmuring stream. Stealing sidelong glances at Elliot, Meera was mesmerized by the way his eyes, now flame-colored, reflected the blazing sky. She sensed a need in him, a pain, a kind of familiar longing. She wanted to make him forget this woman who had meant so much to him. Wanted to be rid of this river of problems that separated them like the creek separated their property. She had to tell him who she was—and she had to do it now.

She drew in a deep breath. "Elliot," she began, "there's something. . ." She stiffened as a new sound reached her ears—the slam of a car door. "Get down," she ordered Elliot in a hoarse whisper, and slid off the rock to the hard ground, crouching low.

Elliot turned his head to look for the source of Meera's concern and saw the car stop in front of the cabin. He ducked and slid down beside Meera, where he peeked through an opening between the rocks. "She's rolling down the window," he whispered.

Louisa's voice rang out loud and clear on the once-peaceful evening air, bringing into play all the bitterness of their deep-rooted hostility and fear. Some very unladylike words rolled off Louisa's tongue, before she added, "I know you're hiding behind those rocks! You dare slither out of there, and I'll blow your head off! Worse than that, I'll—I'll. . ."

"That phony," Elliot said under his breath. "She's sitting in the car, making those empty threats. I ought to go over there and. . ." He balled a fist, glancing at Meera to see her reaction.

Her eyes were wide. She grasped his hand. "Don't chance it! She might have a gun!"

"She's driving away," he reported, still peeking through the small opening.

"She's probably as scared of you as you are of the Briskins."

Seeing that the car was gone, Elliot stood up and scoffed, "Where did you get the idea that I'm scared?"

Meera rose from her crouched position and lifted her chin saucily. "You wouldn't cross the creek last night, and now some frightened female has prevented your slithering out from behind the rocks."

"Always challenging me, aren't you?" he said threateningly. "Maybe, Meera Br. . .Brown. . ." he corrected himself, "maybe I just prefer to choose a more suitable time and place for my demise."

She laughed lightly with him before they both sobered. She could see that he was waiting for her to finish what she had begun before Louisa's arrival had interrupted her. But she chose another tack. "What has a Briskin ever done to you, Elliot? Personally, that is?"

Elliot turned from her questioning eyes, feeling compelled to use caution. Propping his forearms on a boulder, he stared at the cabin, while Meera backed up against the boulders, studying his profile.

Three short days ago, he could have said that the Briskins had remained a thorn in his side only from a distance. Now, however, a Briskin had invaded his private world as surely as the blight had invaded the chestnut trees. Now he was in danger of losing his heart. . .to the enemy!

But aloud he said, "Briskin and Maxwell animosity runs deep, Meera. There's always the feeling that I have to be on guard against them. You heard that girl. Just the thought of a Maxwell turned her into a raving maniac. Well, the Maxwells have the same kind of anger and mistrust just beneath the surface."

"That shouldn't be," she said sadly.

Elliot regarded her with a puzzled frown. Meera Briskin was either entirely sincere or a consummate actress. Why didn't she just tell him the truth about herself and be done with it? But what was the truth? He still didn't know what she was doing here. And what was this thing that had sprung up between them? He felt it, and he knew she did.

He reached for her, and she came into his arms without hesitation. Resting his chin on top of her silvery head, he sighed. "The enmity is so deep. That's why, in the article, you mustn't mention the feud. I'm afraid it might have a bad effect on my dad."

Feeling her tremble, Elliot moved away slightly and looked down into her troubled face. "Can't you tell me what's bothering you?"

She wanted to. But she didn't want to hear his words of disgust. Didn't want to hear all the negative remarks that struck her heart like an arrow each time he mentioned a Briskin.

Too, she kept wondering why Louisa had returned to the cabin. Louisa had made it very clear that she didn't like to be there at night. Perhaps something was wrong at home. She should call. "Now," he prodded gently, giving her every opportunity, "what was it you were about to tell me before we got a prime example of how a Briskin feels about a Maxwell?"

Meera knew she couldn't blurt out her identity here and now—not with all the conflicting emotions still so near the surface. Not with their standing only a few feet away from the spot where Jonas Maxwell had shot her grandfather. But she had to tell him something.

She took a deep breath. "Last night you asked if I was engaged. I'd like to explain about that," she said, a doubtful look crossing her eyes, "if I can. If you want to hear."

"I do," he said, surprised that he was relieved rather than disappointed. Perhaps he was a coward, not wanting to deal with the reality of hearing it from her own lips.

She sat down on a low rock and Elliot sat near her.

"It was a whirlwind romance," she began. "Two summers ago. I met Clark in Venezuela. His family is one-half of Phillips/Coleman Oil."

Seeing Elliot's quick glance and a slight twitch of his mouth, she knew he'd heard of Clark. "You can't believe everything you read in the tabloids," she reminded him curtly.

It was not from the tabloids, but from the more reliable news media that he'd heard it: Clark Phillips—international playboy—linked romantically with numerous socialites and screen stars.

"He swept me off my feet," she confessed, almost apologetically. "But I wanted some kind of proof that I was more to him than his 'reported' exploits."

"Wasn't the proposal and ring proof enough?"

She looked down at her naked finger. "He's been engaged more than once. And now, he's. . .wanting proof that I'm willing to make a more serious commitment."

"Marriage?"

"I. . .don't think so," she said in a small voice.

"And that's why you took off the ring?"

"Not just that. . . ."

"Another woman," he said, guessing correctly.

"I see her as an immature spoiled brat and a conniving flirt who places little value on our friendship," she said adamantly.

"And *that's* when you flew into a jealous rage and threw the ring at him."

"Quite the contrary," she countered. "I was upset, but I waited, thought about it for several days, then calmly removed the ring." She lifted her chin and gave him a sidelong glance. "*Then* I threw it at him."

"But you said you weren't sure. . .about your engagement,"

Elliot prompted.

She sighed. "He persuaded me to—to put the ring back on my finger."

"Mmm," Elliot said, squinting at her finger. "It's pretty small for a guy who's filthy rich."

She gave a weak laugh, but Elliot saw the discomfort in her eyes. "I. . .took it off again while I sort out my feelings. But I am not one to mope around, so I decided to get on with something. . .more worthwhile."

Worthwhile, Elliot thought. The picture she had painted of Clark Phillips struck him as reprehensible. How dare the guy put a price tag on her affections and expect her to prove her love by making a "more serious commitment"—as if he didn't know what that meant! Though, if he were honest, he supposed his own behavior might not appear to be any more exemplary than Clark Phillips'.

"And what 'worthwhile' thing did you decide on?" he asked.

She looked him in the eye. "I decided to come here. . .to the writers' conference."

He regarded her steadily for a long moment. Then, "I'm glad you did."

Her eyes searched his, roaming his face. He wanted to take her in his arms and kiss her again. But he resisted the impulse. Her eyes clouded before she lowered her gaze to the tumbling creek. Apparently she had clammed up again. But why shouldn't she? As far as she could tell, he was no different from her erstwhile fiancé! He hoped he'd have a chance to prove that he was interested in more than her sweet kisses.

Elliot jumped down from the rock and held out his hand. "Meera Brown," he said, "let's go back to the lodge. I have some pictures and information that should be helpful in writing your article."

She smiled, and he added, "Bertha might even give you the

recipe for our famous chestnut dressing." Then he grimaced. "On second thought," he contradicted, "no one's ever been able to pry it out of her with a crowbar."

"Oh, I don't know. She's already talked to me about the macaroon glacés," Meera said, to his astonishment.

"But she wouldn't tell you where we get them!"

She cocked her head in a delightful gesture. "I believe you import them from Italy, sir. Now your secret will be out. Everyone will know those aren't American chestnuts."

He laughed, finding it incredible that a Maxwell and a Briskin could be jesting about such a thing. "Everyone in these parts knows there hasn't been an American chestnut since the 1940s at the latest. What you need is a history lesson, young lady, if you're going to write a decent article about this place."

She was instantly contrite. "Oh, I'd never write anything you wouldn't find acceptable."

He grinned. "I know. 'Subject to my approval.' That was our agreement, wasn't it?"

"I want to make you proud, Elliot Maxwell."

"I hope you will," he murmured under his breath and looked off toward the tennis courts where the conferees were singing now as Josh led them in some old cowboy favorites. "Want to join them?" he asked, indicating the group with a nod of his head.

She shook her head. "Not unless you do. I. . .need to make a phone call."

He sensed she needed privacy. "Use the phone in my office. Then come to the library. The desk clerk can direct you, if you don't know where it is."

In Elliot's office, Meera called the Briskin estate to say that she was fine and still visiting with friends. "That's what your parents have been doing every night this week," Aunt

Clara retorted. "Don't know why we even need this big house. Oh, Louisa just came in. Do you want to talk to her?"

Meera declined. She had nothing to say to her cousin at the moment. Promising to report in again soon, she hung up.

When Meera wandered into the octagonal-shaped library off the main lobby, her footsteps were muffled by the plush carpet, and Elliot didn't look up from his rummaging through a stack of magazines.

Stepping inside the room, she caught the pungent whiff of furniture polish and old leather. Libraries had always fascinated Meera, but this one was particularly inviting with its tapestried couches and chairs, stone fireplace, and roll-top desk. Her eyes were drawn to a portrait hanging above the fireplace. It was a painting of a man and woman, and on first glance, the man appeared to be Elliot. Walking closer, however, she saw that though this person was just as ruggedly handsome, he was much older than Elliot, his dark hair silvering at the temples. The small plaque beneath the gold frame read: "Jonas Elliot Maxwell and Carrie Margaret Spearman."

So this was the woman her grandfather had loved so long ago! The woman, with dark, curly hair and determined deep-blue eyes that reminded her of Elliot's, was the opposite of the pictures Meera had seen of her own grandmother. Her face, though not delicately pretty, was quite attractive with a look of strength. Meera couldn't help thinking that the more gentle woman her grandfather had married was the better choice for him.

She didn't notice Elliot walking up beside her until she felt his fingers at the small of her back.

"My ancestors," he said, wondering how Meera felt, looking at the woman her grandfather had lost through his chicanery.

But as he studied Meera, then his grandmother's portrait,

he had a ridiculous thought. If it had turned out differently, he might be the blond with gray eyes, and she the dark-haired beauty with the very stern expression. . .if the two of them existed at all. He was suddenly glad she did and longed to kiss her and tell her so. But seeing her quizzical look, he resisted the temptation.

"Come over here," he said, changing the subject. "I'd like you to see the video."

Meera watched the brief overview of the Asian fungus that was accidentally introduced into the United States at a time when every fourth tree in the Appalachian forests was an American chestnut. The blight had invaded the trees through its bark, which had developed cankers, identifiable by their orange blush. The spores were then transferred by wind, insects, and birds throughout America, Europe, and Asia.

Threadlike filaments had fanned out and girdled the trees, choking off water and nutrients, until the trees died within months. Nothing was able to stop the blight or control it. Generations fought the blight, spraying, razing, then burying their failed efforts. Within forty years, several billion chestnut trees had been obliterated from the Eastern forests.

Meera learned that the mightiest of the trees were almost seventy feet tall and sixteen feet in circumference. The lumber of one sixty-foot tree would have brought in over five hundred dollars. When sound, the trees had been a favorite for cradles, coffins, telegraph and telephone poles, and fence posts because of the wood's weather-and rot-resistance. Its three brown nuts, nestled in sable-soft downy fur and protected by a sticky burr, was food for squirrel, deer, bear, wild turkey, and people.

When a tree was cut, it grew back from the roots—and after the blight struck, so did the cankers. The brave new growth struggled fiercely for survival, but soon withered and died.

"Surely you don't blame the Briskins for that," she said, wiping a tear from her eye at the dismal spectacle.

"Of course not," he replied immediately. "Just for selling the land to my granddad, knowing that the trees were blighted."

"And suppose the Briskins didn't know?"

He stared at her. "Elias Briskin knew." But she looked so downcast that Elliot felt compelled to add, "At least, that's what my granddad believed."

The next footage showed the building of Chestnut Lodge. Wings were added onto the main house, utilizing as much of the good chestnut lumber as possible, and given the name Chestnut Lodge, in memory of a bygone glory.

When the video rolled to an end, Elliot pushed the rewind button. "My ancestors nearly lost their shirt in that deal," Elliot said, striking fear to her heart, "but my grandfather always thought he lost something more valuable. . .and that was a lifelong friendship with Elias Briskin."

Meera knew that any rebuttal she might make would not be believed. Three generations of animosity and misunderstanding couldn't be erased with a few words. But she would keep trying to find a way.

Maybe one of these days, Elliot thought, he'd have an opportunity to remind her that he hadn't even been born when Jonas Maxwell shot Elias Briskin—and that she hadn't been around when Briskin sold the blighted land to the Maxwells. But for now, he focused on her upcoming article, giving her some tips and loading her down with with resource materials. Because it seemed to be so important to her, he'd begun to want her to do a good job on the article. And when the evening wound down, he prided himself on having behaved like a gentleman.

Rising to go, she stood framed in the doorway, her shiny hair swinging softly against her shoulders as her lovely face turned toward his. "I want you to know that I'm not on the rebound, Elliot," she informed him seriously. "When you kiss me, I don't even know Clark Phillips exists."

To his chagrin, while he was still halfway across the room, clinging to the back of a chair to resist the impulse to rush to her side, she smiled sweetly and disappeared into the lobby.

seven

"I'll make you proud," Meera had promised last night, and she began making good on that promise from the moment she put in an appearance early the next morning at the breakfast buffet.

Elliot knew he was seeing more than Meera Brown, fledgling writer, uncertain of her skills and her relationship with him. He was glimpsing Meera Briskin, the polished young woman—educated, intelligent, confident.

"May I join you?" she asked, coming up to the table where Elliot and Harold Wright sat discussing the conference.

More than once, Elliot had observed Harold advising a student to make an appointment through the registrar, or to wait until a break when he might have a few minutes. But this time the conference director surprised him. Harold brightened and rose to acknowledge the beautiful young woman in her crisp beige linen business suit, her hair pulled back in a no-nonsense twist.

"Oh, don't let me interrupt if you're discussing business. Mine can wait."

"Not at all," Harold replied. "I think Elliot and I have finished, haven't we?"

Elliot's lips twitched almost imperceptibly. "If you'll excuse me."

"Oh, this involves you both." Meera flashed him a smile brighter than the morning sunshine streaming through the dining room windows.

"Could I get you something to eat?" Elliot asked with

concern.

She was opening her notebook. "A bran muffin and a glass of orange juice, please."

He motioned for one of the servers, gave her the order, then deliberately allowed his eyes to linger on Meera's lips. The only indication that she had noticed was the slight flutter of her lashes and the becoming shade of pink that rose to her cheeks.

She turned her attention to Harold. "May I interview you, Mr. Wright, and include information about the conference in my article on Chestnut Lodge?"

"Of course! That is, if Elliot agrees. After all, it's his lodge." Harold glanced over to Elliot for confirmation.

Elliot spread his hands. "It's your conference."

Harold was wise enough to know that the publicity would have the potential to boost his conference, both in enrollment and prestige. Apparently, Elliot thought, whatever Meera B. asked of him, he would deliver. And she began to present her requests, in her gentle, but intelligent manner. Considerate of his time, she asked nothing that she could obtain from brochures, and before the hour had ended, she had managed to secure some excellent quotes from Harold, along with his promise to put his photographer to work for her. Then she made several appointments for ten minutes each—with Elliot and his staff, including his day manager and the chef—working around the "Advanced Interviews" session and the "Inspirational" workshop she yet wanted to attend.

When Meera had finished, she thanked them and followed the photographer into the kitchen while other students were making their way to Rhododendron Hall for the large group session. "I'm surprised to hear that she's just a beginner with only three articles published," Harold told Elliot. "She knows her way around an interview." He frowned. "Too bad she didn't enter anything in our competitions."

"I have her articles in my office," Elliot suggested. "Would they do?"

"I'll take a look. Come by during the break." With a nod, Harold was off to introduce the morning speaker.

Later, in Elliot's office, leafing through several issues of *Fabulous Places*, Harold paused to read Meera's articles. Elliot detected a wistful note in the director's voice when he commented, "Not just anybody can get published in this magazine."

He returned the material to the folder. "Faculty members normally recommend names for Most Promising Student. I usually stay out of it."

Harold appeared to be debating with himself. Then he grasped the envelope tightly. "I suppose as director, I *could* recommend someone. We have several entries, so I'll pass this around to the judges."

By noon, Elliot realized he was keenly anticipating the upcoming banquet. For one thing, he was looking forward to seeing Trevor again. And then there was the possibility of seeing Meera win an award. It was an altogether pleasant thought.

Although his staff was perfectly capable, Elliot himself personally inspected Rhododendron Hall, where the banquet would be held. Set beneath the vaulted cathedral ceiling were tall panes of glass so clear it seemed he could reach out and touch the lush foliage dappled by the afternoon sunshine.

Inside, the hardwood floor was polished to a glossy sheen, and three hundred wooden folding chairs with leather seats and backs were arranged in rows on each side of a center aisle. The podium, where Trevor would speak, stood on a platform. Behind it was a small table where awards would await some well-deserving conferees.

"Testing, testing," he said over the microphone and adjusted the sound. At the back of the room was a chestnut table where the conference bookstore would display Trevor's books. He would be available to autograph them after his speech.

Surveying the room, Elliot smiled with satisfaction. The staff had outdone themselves. Everything was perfect. The main topic of their conversation as they set up chairs and polished silver was Meera's proposed article about the lodge. Their names might be mentioned. Some of them might even appear in the candid shots taken by the photographer to illustrate the piece.

Others had taken note of the special attention Elliot had paid Meera. And since the first day she walked into Chestnut Lodge, Tom had worn a perpetual grin.

The conference would end tonight. She would have to tell him about her deception tonight—if she intended to tell him at all. Or at the latest. . .in the morning.

Suddenly realizing how quickly time was passing, Elliot went into the alcove and turned up the dimmer lights, for it would be dark outside when the group came in for their closing session. The air would cool quickly after the sun went down, but with a crowd of people in the room, they wouldn't need heat. He turned the ceiling fans on low for circulation.

In the formal dining room, staff members were setting up the tables. Overlays of cream-colored lace topped skirts the color of winter rhododendron leaves, enhanced by goldware and dark green napkins embossed with the "CL" emblem in one corner. To block out the early evening light when they ate, the drapes would be drawn, the great chandelier dimmed, and on each table the short cream candles in golden holders would be lighted to lend an air of cozy elegance. No detail had been overlooked.

Everything seemed to be proceeding on schedule, with not

a hitch. Even when Elliot was summoned to the desk to take a call, there was no warning of impending trouble.

But the smile left his face and the satisfaction in his eyes turned to distress when he heard his dad's voice. "Son, your mother and I are coming to the Lodge tonight to hear Trevor."

"But the doctor said. . ."

"The doctor said no work," Max interrupted, "and I don't intend to work. I'm going to stick to my diet—no fat, no cholesterol—so I'll skip the prime rib and the chocolate mousse and eat my salad. Just wanted to let you know we'd be there."

Elliot felt as if all the air had left his lungs. His folks were coming. With a Briskin on the premises!

But. . .they wouldn't know her. Would they?

Suddenly he felt as if he'd eaten that forbidden fruit. . .and it had turned out to be a little sour green apple. He could feel the consequences beginning to churn in his stomach.

≈

It had been a busy morning. Now, during afternoon free time, Meera pointed her silver bullet toward the Briskin estate. She'd need something special to wear for the banquet.

Never had a spring been so beautiful. Never had she felt so alive! So fulfilled. She was accomplishing something on her own. Well, not exactly on her own. But her dependence upon her grandfather—his presence, his advice, his love, his faith—had always been so much a part of her. She had felt so lost without him. But now, she could remember him with joy instead of pain.

And this thing with Elliot Maxwell. Well, it was going to work out. It just had to. He was an intelligent person. He would understand perfectly why she had felt compelled to conceal her identity. It wouldn't matter.

The inspirational classes had helped too. Not just with her writing, but in defining problems and finding solutions through prayer and seeking the wisdom of God. The instructor was a very strong Christian who had emphasized her own faith and pointed out the place of divine inspiration in writing. Meera felt like the faith of her grandfather was becoming more solidly her own.

Yes, there were a few things to work out, but Meera had every confidence that, if she handled them the right way, these could be accomplished without anyone being hurt. The last sessions had been very revealing, and she was proud of her actions during the morning when she had pushed her insecurities aside and dared act like a writer who knew what she was doing. It had worked! She had felt thoroughly professional. Truly this conference had given her a new direction.

Not only that, but miracle of miracles, Elliot Maxwell liked her! She would have to tell him tonight. She dared not think beyond that.

"Woooo-oooo Woooo-oooo Woooo-ooooo!"

The sound finally registered, and Meera looked in the rearview mirror to see a flashing blue light. She gripped the steering wheel. Then, as if some kind of automaton took over, she obediently pulled over to the side of the road.

Her heart was beating even faster when the officer got out of his squad car and walked up to the window. A pad and pencil were in his hands.

Oh, no! Elliot must have discovered her identity and was having her arrested for trespassing! Was that really possible? Maybe a charge couldn't stick, but obviously an arrest could be made. The officer lowered his head and peered at her over a pair of non-existent eyeglasses.

It would be plastered all over the papers. Her reputation would be ruined, not to mention her relationship with her family. And Elliot—would he really do such a thing? Yes, came the answer from deep within. He was a Maxwell, wasn't he!

"Ma'am," the officer growled, "did you know you're driving down the Blue Ridge Parkway?"

"Y—yessir," she stuttered.

"Do you know the speed limit on the Parkway?"

Was she going to get a speeding ticket? Not be arrested for trespassing or falsifying information? "F—forty-five?"

"Then why were you doing fifty-five?"

"I'm sorry," she said. "I guess I was preoccupied. I just didn't think about the speed."

"What are you so happy about? Is it your birthday or something?"

Meera laughed lightly. "No, sir," and even as she answered, realization was dawning. "I understand you have to give me a ticket."

He quirked his brow. "So this isn't your first one?"

"Oh, it is! But I know you're just doing your job."

"Well. . .consider this a warning, little lady. You keep speeding and you won't have any more birthdays."

"I understand," she said. "And thank you."

He walked back to his car and waited until she pulled out onto the road again.

My birthday! she thought, keeping her eye on the speedometer. *Oh, it's better than that. It was a new-birth day! A new beginning!* Little niggling doubts clawed at her when she reached home, however. Hearing the TV, she realized she hadn't seen one in days, nor had she read a newspaper. She had been in a different world for the past few days, a fantasy world—just Elliot Maxwell's and hers.

She would have to return to reality soon. But she had one more night, and she would make the best of it. Peeking into the study, she saw Louisa lying on the couch watching the soaps.

"Well, so you decided to come home!"

"Nope," Meera countered. "Just came for a party dress."

Louisa began her third-degree again, but Meera hastened on to her bedroom. As she figured, her cousin was too wrapped up in the story to follow.

Meera thought of calling Cathy Steinbord and telling her to ask Trevor not to reveal her identity, if he knew it. But she decided against it. She shouldn't be dragging other people into this.

The dress she chose was a white shimmery satin that she'd worn to the ambassador's dinner party in Venezuela the last time she was there. A row of small Briskin rubies, alternating with silver sequins, bordered the V-neckline. The skirt flounced daintily from a small waistline and fell to just above her knees. She would wear it with matching shoes—a silver iridescent sling with a white satin high heel. At the last minute, she grabbed her favorite earrings—a delicate cascade of small rubies and silver dangles.

As she recalled, the outfit had made a big impression on the ambassador. She wondered what Elliot would think. Suddenly his approval seemed more important than all the ambassadors in the world!

❧

Meera hoped to see Trevor Steinbord as soon as he arrived for the banquet. He probably wouldn't remember meeting her, but if he did, he might recall that she was a Briskin, and she couldn't chance her name slipping out inadvertently in conversation. Since he was a friend of Elliot's, she'd have to tell him that she was using her pseudonym here at the conference. Like everyone else in the area, he would surely understand that she wouldn't want a Maxwell to know that a Briskin was on his property. She'd simply have to intercept him before Elliot did.

Having met Trevor at Chapel Hill, Meera knew that his

blond head could always be seen several inches above that of the tallest person in the room. He was certainly something to look at, but after she and several of her college friends had read his first book, *Undivided*, they had concluded that he was pining away for some mystery woman who could never be his. The air of intrigue made him appealing, but put him slightly out of reach—the kind of man one tended to admire from a distance.

Elliot was nowhere in sight when Meera entered the lobby and moved toward the sweeping windows across the front of the building. Soon, a long black Lincoln Continental pulled up and parked in front. A tall, classically handsome man got out, closed the door, and fastened the buttons of his suit coat, then ran one hand across his blond hair. Trevor Steinbord!

So engrossed was Meera in her inspection that she almost forgot she had intended to corner him before he could speak to Elliot. Now, however, she realized that the conference director and several faculty members had also been waiting to see him and, as soon as he entered the door, Trevor was surrounded.

Meera's heart stood still while he spoke to the group, then shrugged aside his professional air and walked over to greet Elliot, who was standing near the registration desk. To her horror, Elliot spotted her, and the two moved in her direction.

"You remember Meera Brown?" Elliot asked, watching Trevor closely for signs of recognition.

A polite smile touched Trevor's lips, but Meera could see the confusion in his eyes. "Oh, he probably doesn't," Meera said quickly, extending her hand. "Your sister Cathy introduced us several years ago when you spoke to our journalism class at Chapel Hill."

"Meera Brown," Trevor said, shaking her hand. "Cathy mentioned that you visited in our home a couple of times."

So he did remember! "Yes, but you were out of the country, I believe," she responded with a smile.

Elliot saw the eye contact between the two—Trevor's, guarded; hers, pleading not to be betrayed.

While this little scenario was being played out, Harold Wright came over and touched Trevor on the arm. "If you'll follow me, I'll show you to the head table."

"Nice meeting you again, Miss. . .Brown," Trevor said, then glanced quickly at his friend. "Hope to see you later, Elliot."

"Sure thing." Elliot knew that Trevor Steinbord could mask his true feelings better than anyone he'd ever known. But he also knew that since Trevor remembered having met Meera in his parents' home, he must also remember that she was a Briskin.

At least, he'd covered for her when Elliot introduced them. And Elliot was grateful to him for that. As grateful as Meera must be. That confession should come from her—and no one else.

Meera glanced at Elliot and gave him a tentative smile.

He winked. "Did I tell you how beautiful you look tonight?"

She shook her head. "Thanks. So do you."

"Well, I'd like to pursue this line of thought," he said with a grin, "but I need to open the dining room doors and greet my other guests." He hurried away with one last lingering look at Meera.

❧

Elliot mingled with the conferees, noting the aura of celebration that pervaded the atmosphere. It had been a successful conference, and everyone seemed upbeat. After greeting the guests and checking in with the kitchen staff to be sure everything was proceeding on schedule, Elliot filled his plate from the kitchen and joined his parents, who had arrived without fanfare, at a small table nearby.

"Who was that young woman?" his mother wanted to know immediately.

"What young woman?" Elliot asked innocently.

"The pretty blonde you and Trevor were talking to in the lobby."

Elliot pretended thoughtfulness. "Oh," he said as if suddenly remembering, "she's someone he met through Cathy. Well, Dad, how am I doing here?"

"I can't say as far as the pretty girls are concerned, son. . . ." Max Maxwell laughed at his own joke. "But you seem to have everything else at the lodge under control. Harold's happy, the place looks great, and this is the best London broil I've ever eaten."

His wife smacked him playfully on the hand. "That's because you haven't eaten anything like that in months, Max, and you're not supposed to be eating it now. Put that down!"

"Now, Mother, a bite or two won't hurt. I know what I'm doing."

Elliot couldn't very well reprimand his father. That "pretty blonde" he'd allowed to stay on Maxwell property for the past few days was enough to give anyone heart problems. He'd just have to make sure they didn't meet. But if they did, he'd try and pass her off as Trevor's friend.

After the banquet, Elliot sat at the back of Rhododendron Hall where the staff could signal him if he were needed. His parents sat next to him. Normally, they would not sit in on a session, but they were eager to hear Trevor's speech. As expected, it was quite impressive.

He watched his friend—the suave, handsome, renowned novelist—weaving his spell over his audience. Only his family and a few close friends knew that he'd written his first book at a very early age, out of an aching heart over a lost love. The book had made him famous. Only in an occasional private moment did Trevor let his guard down, but the pain and pathos showed through, creating an instant rapport with his listeners. Elliot understood that kind of pain. Maybe that's why he and Trevor had remained friends, though they rarely saw each other anymore.

Typical of Trevor, once he had gained the full support of his audience, he turned their attention to God, Who gifts people with creativity and drive and expects them to develop and use those gifts to the best of their ability.

Elliot's reverie was broken by a wave of deafening applause, and he stood to acknowledge the speaker, along with the students and faculty.

When they sat down for the closing ceremonies, Elliot remained rather than leaving to check on the front desk. Knowing there was more to come, he felt the quickening of his pulse. He smoothed his silk tie, tugged at the lapels of his dark blue suit, and brushed an imaginary speck of lint from his pants.

When Harold Wright rose to announce the awards, Elliot's anticipation mounted. Several awards were presented—Most Improved Writer, Best Juvenile Entry, Best Young Adult Entry, Best Adult Entry. Then it was time for the most coveted award of all—Most Promising Writer.

Elliot's heart was in his throat when Harold called out at last, "Meera Brown."

He glanced over to see her reaction. Meera was obviously shocked, and her name had to be called a second time. A red-headed girl seemed to be assuring her that she had indeed won the award. With hands to her flaming cheeks, Meera left her seat and hurried up the aisle toward the front, where Harold stood at the microphone, holding an engraved silver cup.

Elliot was stunned when she took the microphone and began to speak. And his enchantment had little to do the illusion of angelic beauty she presented in her white dress studded with stones that winked and sparkled as it caught the light. He'd come to believe that Meera Brown—at least a part of her—was a beautiful, capable person. For the next few minutes, she proved him right.

"For one of the few times in my life, I don't know what to say," she began and the audience laughed kindly.

She spoke quickly, emotionally, swiping at the liquid joy that filled her eyes. "I don't know if you can imagine what this means to me. . . ." she said and paused. "No, that's not true. I suppose, being writers, you can imagine *anything*." Her audience laughed again, appreciatively. "I didn't know I needed an award, or even wanted one," she said to Harold Wright who was beaming his approval of her, "but I did, and I do, and I'll try to live up to it."

Elliot thought about the professionalism she had displayed last night in his office when they'd finally gotten down to the interview, then again this morning. Now, he watched as she shook Harold's hand and hurried straight down the aisle toward the back of the room, amid applause and Harold's announcement that Trevor would be autographing books in the front lobby, where the conference would host a reception for him.

In the excitement, Elliot had completely forgotten his parents. Too late, he realized he should have ducked out the moment Meera left the stage. She was making a beeline for him.

"I know I'm acting like an idiot," she said, when she came up to Elliot and regarded him through cloudy eyes.

He shook his head.

She held out the cup for him to see. "This is like confirmation that I'm becoming my own person, apart from family. Oh, Elliot, I know you must have had something to do with this. . .and I love you for it," she choked out.

He saw the terror that leapt into her eyes at this slip. But he couldn't let her stand there with her success falling down around her ankles like an old sock. "Well, I rate tonight," he said, hating the thinness he heard in his voice. "One of my secretaries told me she loved my tie."

Thankfully someone grasped Meera's arm and dragged her off to receive congratulations from other fellow conferees just as he noticed his parents staring at him as if he were the boogie-man. He left the room before they could accost him.

The word was used much too casually, almost blithely, he mused. Writers, of all people, should know that. *I love your tie. I love that song. Some people even love broccoli.*

"Mr. Elliot. Your daddy never frowned at my reception tables like that," came a disdainful wail, and he turned to see Bertha with sparks in her eyes hotter than the candles she'd just lighted.

"Oh, Bertha, there you are. I was just on my way to look for you. . . ." he began as he walked with her toward the dining room, knowing he'd spend the next thirty minutes trying to placate her.

Elliot couldn't very well say his daddy would do more than frown if he knew the real truth about the situation here. More than likely, his dad would say that there was only one thing worse than feuding with a Briskin. . .and that would be *not* feuding with one!

eight

Before Trevor left, he stopped by Elliot's office and tapped on the door. "Just wanted to say that it's good being back at Chestnut Lodge and seeing you again, Elliot," he said, poking his head into the room. "Saw your parents too. Glad your dad's getting along all right."

"Thanks, pal. Come on in and have a seat." Eliot motioned to the chairs in front of the fireplace, then went over and sat opposite Trevor. "I want an autographed copy of that new book before you leave."

Trevor nodded. They chatted briefly about his travels and his next writing project. Then Elliot broached the subject that was uppermost on his mind. "What do you think of her?"

"Very attractive. . .gifted. . .interesting." Trevor grinned, his blue eyes twinkling. "I got the impression there's something going on between the two of you."

"We—ll, you know she's a Briskin." From Trevor's noncommittal look, Elliot could see that the statement didn't surprise him. Of course, he knew about the feud. "I'm afraid it may be an impossible situation."

The veil that Elliot knew so well fell over his friend's face. Trevor had his own impossible situation—loving a woman he couldn't have—so he'd poured his heart and soul into his writing. "I suppose it comes down to this," Trevor said pointedly. "What exactly do you want out of this relationship?"

Leave it to Trevor to get right to the point. He knew what and who he wanted and had resigned himself to the fact that it could never happen. So, he often appeared at public functions

107

with beautiful women on his arm who understood that there would be no long-term, serious commitment.

With Elliot, it hadn't been that easy—or that difficult. Kate was dead. But he supposed Trevor had nailed it down. What *did* he want from Meera?

"I'm not sure," Elliot mused aloud, "that there *is* a relationship, Trevor. I think she may be playing some kind of game."

Trevor lifted a brow. "Have you agreed to the ground rules?"

Elliot laughed wryly. "Yes and no. I'm beginning to feel like a compulsive gambler who's losing his shirt and then becomes so desperate to win that he goes deeper and deeper in debt."

"There's a major difference, Elliot," Trevor said after a thoughtful moment. "With a compulsive gambler, the odds are in favor of the casino, or the fall of the cards. Here, I'd say, the odds are pretty much even."

"In some ways," Elliot admitted. When it came to family, Meera had as much to lose as he. Her family would not approve her being here—unless it was a deliberate set-up of some kind.

Trevor made a suggestion. "Maybe you should look at it as a challenge, not a gamble."

"What you say makes sense," Elliot agreed, but met Trevor's steady gaze with one of his own. "But what makes sense when it comes to emotions?"

Trevor jabbed his thumb in his chest. "Look who's giving advice," he said with irony. "Of our friends, Josh is the psychologist."

"And all he did was shrug his shoulders and wink at me," Elliot said, laughing.

The companionable smile faded from Trevor's face. "When it comes to matters of the heart, Elliot, advice doesn't help much. We're pretty much on our own in that department."

Elliot stood. "You going to be around for a while?"

Trevor nodded. "A few days. Give me a call. Maybe we can get together. Double date?"

Elliot saw the mischief in the blue eyes and knew without a doubt his friend was aware that a Maxwell couldn't be seen in public around here with a Briskin. It would be sure to make the front page of the newspaper and provide fodder for local TV talk shows. Besides, no place was private when in the company of the famous Trevor Steinbord. "Thanks a lot!" Elliot intoned with playful sarcasm.

Trevor laughed. "At least you know what you're up against."

"Fortunately," Elliot said, then added, "I think."

Trevor's parting words were succinct. "When you find something in life you want, Elliot, and if it doesn't hurt anyone else, then go for it."

Elliot knew the other side of that coin. If it was possible that someone would be hurt, then step out of the picture—as Trevor had.

Later, after his parents came by the office to say they were leaving, Elliot walked out back, past a few milling guests, thinking about his conversation with his successful friend. Trevor had pursued his second love—writing. *Suppose Meera is first on my want list,* Elliot thought, *there are certainly those people who would stand to be hurt if I go after her.* But if not, must he revert to fear, mistrust, and animosity toward her and all her family—people he would have continued to write off if she hadn't come here, dispelling forever the myth that all Briskins were cut out of the same cloth?

No! He couldn't go back. The Briskins were no longer mere legend. Now they were personified in the form of a very lovely and desirable blonde. Perhaps Meera had devious motives.

Even so, she was an innocent victim, the same as he, of the venomous feud that had been bequeathed to them.

He walked down the steps from the deck. Now that the conference was over, would she leave without an explanation? Without revealing her identity? Or had she really only come here to pursue a writing career? Elliot sighed deeply. If so, she had accomplished her purpose.

&a

As the evening wound down, most of the local conferees left the lodge for home. Others gathered to talk in small groups or to stroll the gardens one last time. Meera took her award cup to her room, then went in search of Elliot. When she didn't find him in his office, she walked out back.

The determined click of her heels against the stone patio came to an abrupt halt when she stumbled upon Elliot who glanced at her, said, "Shh," and put his finger to his lips. She cautiously tiptoed to where he stood gazing up into a young dogwood tree.

"Look," he whispered, and her gaze followed his as she peered up into the spreading branches of delicate white blossoms against a bright moonlit sky.

His arm came around her shoulders. Startled, she looked into his face.

"Do you see it?" he asked.

Yes, she saw it. She saw the determined chin, the strong jawline, the firm full lips that had taken possession of hers, just as he had taken possession of her heart. "Right here," he said and she looked again.

Just when she began to suspect he was playing a silly game, she saw it. "Ohh, how beautiful," she breathed. "I've never seen anything like that."

Hanging from a low branch of the dogwood tree was a cocoon, from which a butterfly was emerging. Involuntarily, her hand came up as if to caress it.

"Don't touch," Elliot warned. "It's still wet. One touch can impair or even destroy its ability to fly."

"You remind me of my grandfather," Meera said wistfully. "He taught me so much about nature. But I've never seen a butterfly leaving its home. I didn't know it was such a tedious chore."

"Like humans in some ways," Elliot pondered. "Breaking family ties is difficult. Family is the strongest bond we have."

Staring at the butterfly, she thought of his words. How wise he was. Even though her family might be wrong in their attitude toward the Maxwells, she still felt a fierce loyalty toward them, that obligatory bond of blood.

She turned her face toward his. "I know. I love my family, Elliot. My dad gave me the silver convertible for my birthday. But. . .that little silver cup tonight meant more. . . ."

He nodded in understanding. "You earned it. No one could buy it for you. That makes all the difference."

"Then you must feel this kind of accomplishment in what you do here at the lodge."

Elliot narrowed his gaze, squinting into the night. "There's nothing out there for me that can compare with these mountains. This is my own little niche."

She drew in a breath of the pure crystalline air, perfumed with the scent of mountain laurel and calacanthus and pine, so different from the Venezuelan oil fields. "I wanted to tell you," she said, "that I appreciate the way you handled the interview."

Elliot shrugged, puzzled. "It was you who handled it."

"Yes, but you kept things on a strictly businesslike basis."

"That's what you wanted, wasn't it?"

"Exactly," Meera replied, not daring to meet his eyes.

He lifted her chin with his finger until she was forced to

look at him. "You thought I'd get personal?"

She smiled and nodded. It occurred to her that she had come here to discover whether or not she could respect a Maxwell. When had the tables turned? When had it become so important that a Maxwell respect a Briskin?

"I saw a professional side of you, Meera. And I was impressed."

"You know something, Elliot Maxwell," she said, cocking her head to one side. "I. . .I like you."

She had thought he might reciprocate, but when he didn't, she was grateful for the cloak of near-darkness that concealed the rush of heat to her face. She forced her attention back to the butterfly. "Will the little creature be okay?"

He stared a moment longer, then he looked up into the tree. "It takes hours for a butterfly to emerge. But eventually it will break free of that inhibiting cocoon and. . ." He lowered his voice, "And fly away."

A long moment passed before he faced her again and asked softly, "Are you going to fly away, Meera Brown?"

She closed her eyes and bit on her lip. She wished she were really Meera Brown. But she had been as slow to leave that pseudonym behind her as the butterfly was to release itself from the cocoon. Her wings had been touched. Elliot Maxwell's fingerprints were on them. She would much rather make love than war.

"There's something I have to tell you, Elliot. Something that will make you despise me."

His pulse quickened. She was going to confess at last. They could get her little deception out of the way and honestly explore their feelings for each other. If they wanted to put an end to the Maxwell-Briskin feud, they could do it. . . together.

He wanted her to be honest with him. And in that moment of being honest with himself, a shocking realization dawned:

He wanted more of Meera Brown—Meera Briskin—than a few stolen kisses.

"First," she said, and he heard the reluctance in her voice, saw the fear in her eyes, "promise me you'll hear me out . . ." she swallowed hard but did not look away, "before you condemn me."

"I promise." It was all he could do to suppress the flood of joy that coursed through his veins. *Darling*, he was thinking, *if you don't like your last name, we'll change it!* By George, there were more important things to consider than that stupid feud.

He found himself enjoying this little charade of his. There was enough Maxwell in him to feel a sense of satisfaction over her discomfort. Someday they could perhaps laugh about it. But for now, he deliberately pasted a frown on his face and tried to furrow his brow as he snorted, "You're married! Is that it? Is that the reason for this white circle around your finger?"

"No, no," she said quickly.

"Divorced?"

She shook her head, and the little sparks in her gray eyes reflected the twinkling stars in the velvet sky.

"So you're engaged after all!" he said and placed his hand on his forehead.

She laughed at his antics, loving his playfulness, knowing he was trying to make it easier for her to come forth with a confession.

"I do have to think about that part," she said, "the engagement, I mean."

"I can deal with that." She could not possibly think Clark Phillips was right for her.

Meera glanced around, realizing that the place was suddenly deserted and that she and Elliot were alone. She breathed deeply of the cool, fragrant night air and lifted her eyes again to the butterfly whose wings had emerged a little further. How long before it would fly away?

She looked at Elliot again. Not knowing any subtle way to do this, she plunged in. "What is the worst thing you could think about me?"

A few days ago, he would have responded instantly, "Being a Briskin." Instead, he said, "You're an ax murderer!"

She giggled in spite of the gravity of the moment. "Oh, Elliot, be serious!" Then she sobered. "I wish it were that simple."

"Wait," he said, lifting his hand in a gesture of protest. "Before you say anything else, I want you to know. . ." With his fingers he touched the moonlight on her face, traced a pattern across her mouth, gently drew her closer. Then he bent his head and let his lips say it for him.

Meera knew this could be the last time he ever held her, and she put her arms around his neck and ran her fingers through the hair that curled at the back of his head, returning his kisses with a warmth that surprised her.

At last Elliot moved away, managing to say huskily, "I've never wanted anyone in my arms as much as I want you."

"I've never felt quite this way before either," Meera said earnestly, "but I have to tell you. . .now. . .or I'll never be able to."

Suddenly, Elliot wanted no more games, no more delays. *Say it and be done with it,* he was thinking, and grabbed her hand, bringing her fingers to his lips. Then he pulled her close once more, cradling her head on his chest. "You can tell me anything, don't you know that?"

"Elliot," she said in a whisper, trembling, both from the impact of his thorough kisses and the confession she must now give, a confession that could change everything between them. "I'm. . ."

But the next words he heard came from a different source.

"Well, well! This is quite an exhibition. Looks like you're not the only one who walks in at unexpected times, huh, Meera?"

Meera whirled to face her cousin, who looked as smug and satisfied as the cat who swallowed the canary. "Louisa!" she gasped, grateful at least that the young woman had not divulged her last name. It would never do for Elliot to hear it from someone else. "Wh—What what are you doing here?"

Louisa laughed, lifting her lovely face toward the sky. "That's really not important. What *is* important is that *I* know what *you're* doing here," she said in a silky voice. "Apparently, you're hang gliding from the Maxwell mountains."

Meera glanced at Elliot's troubled face. Oh, no! He would recognize Louisa from last night! He had seen her at the Briskin cabin. The old fear rose up, suffocating her. He might just shoot them both!

Louisa was backing away, as if the full implication of what she was doing had just occurred to her.

"I'll explain later," Meera said over her shoulder to Elliot and reached for Louisa, grasping her arm. "Let's get out of here."

"Hold it!" Elliot shouted.

They stopped dead in their tracks, and Elliot read the alarm in their faces. Served them right. Maxwells could play games as well as Briskins. Two of them now! Okay, he'd play along. "Haven't I seen you somewhere before?" he asked, walking closer, scrutinizing the girl.

Louisa shook her head, her eyes wild with fear.

"Aren't you the nightmare on Briskin property who threatened to shoot me last night? Who are you? What do you want?"

Louisa looked from Elliot to Meera and pointed a shaking finger at Meera. "Well, she's. . ."

Before she could finish, Elliot directed his remarks to Meera. "I'm calling the police! Or better yet, I'll deal with this in my own way. Never let it be said that a Maxwell doesn't know how to handle a Briskin!"

He rushed past them and hurried into the lodge.

"This is awful, Louisa," Meera said fearfully. "He doesn't know who I am."

"Ohh, he's going after a shotgun. I know it!" Louisa wailed, rocking back and forth on her high heels.

"Then get out of here. I'll meet you at the cabin."

Louisa took off up the steep drive and ran around the lodge.

It served her right, Meera thought, then added to herself, *Serves me right too.*

ఎ

Elliot stood beside the window in his darkened office and watched the frightened woman jump into the black sportscar parked in front of the lodge. She fumbled nervously with the key, then started the engine, and roared out of the drive.

With this incident, a new insight was surfacing, Elliot mused. It seemed the Briskin clan felt more fear than hatred for the Maxwells. At least, this was true of two of them.

Gloating inwardly, he relished a small sense of triumph. At last he had the upper hand. Now, Meera Briskin would be at his mercy. He waited for a few minutes, then called her room.

He heard her intake of breath before she answered in a faint voice, "Hello?"

"I think we should talk," he said seriously, hoping she would not detect the enjoyment he was experiencing or the relief he felt that this charade woud finally be over and they could get on to more pleasurable things.

"In the morning?" she asked weakly.

"Now," he said with mock severity. "Privately, of course. Would you come to my suite, please?"

His suite? She blinked back the moisture in her eyes. Before now, she might have insisted upon a more appropriate meeting place for their confrontation. But now it didn't matter. He wouldn't try anything. It was too late for that. Louisa had ruined any hope of a reconciliation between the Briskins and the Maxwells.

Louisa? No! Meera had no one to blame but herself. "Give me a few minutes," she begged.

Yes! He could wait. . .for a few minutes.

He hung up and smiled at the telephone. In a "few minutes," it would all be over. They could declare a truce.

≈

When she didn't show up in twenty minutes, he knew.

He went through the motions anyway. First, he called her room. The phone just kept ringing. He was tired of the game that was no longer a game.

He went to her door and knocked. He would make it easy for her. He'd tell her the truth: that he had known from the beginning. Then he'd take her in his arms and console her, convince her that everything would be all right.

But she didn't answer. He used his pass key, half expecting to find her slumped on the bed, crying with remorse—sorry that she had deceived him, asking his forgiveness. His pulse quickened at the thought.

He opened the door, calling her name. There was no answer. No sobbing. No tearful, "Go away."

He switched on the light. There was no Meera. He went into the bedroom. No sign of anything. The bed was made just as room service would have left it that morning. In the closet, there were no suitcases. Only an extra blanket on the top shelf.

The bathroom door was open. She wouldn't be in there. He looked anyway.

The last futile effort was to go out onto the balcony. Nothing—but a dark Briskin mountain looming ominously ahead like a barrier flung against the sky. A cold breeze struck him in the face and went straight to his heart.

She hadn't even said good-bye.

He dragged himself through the lonely rooms once more. Then his gaze fell on the phone. He lifted the receiver and called the front desk. The night clerk answered.

"Did Miss Meera Brown check out?"

"Yes, sir."

"How long ago?"

"Ten. . .fifteen minutes. Anything wrong?"

"No," Elliot lied. "Everything's fine."

A few minutes later he walked out toward the parking lot where she'd parked the silver convertible. The spot was empty. There would be no more Meera Brown/Briskin. She'd apparently accomplished what she'd come for—whatever that was.

Maybe it really was to hone her writing skills. Maybe it was to hear the famous Trevor Steinbord. Maybe it was to avenge her family honor by breaking a Maxwell's heart.

She had accomplished one positive thing. He would no longer brood over Kate. That was done—over—finished, although he would always cherish her memory.

Coming back toward the lodge, Elliot neared the dogwood tree and stopped to see the progress of the butterfly. It was gone. It had flown away.

Head bent, hands shoved into his pants pockets, Elliot stared at the ground in front of him as he returned to the lodge.

He didn't hate Meera Briskin. But she had closed the door to his loving her. He would simply forget her.

nine

"It didn't mean anything. It was a mistake," Meera said defensively when Louisa hurled the expected accusations in her face.

You see," Louisa crowed triumphantly, holding the screen door open while Meera passed through with her suitcases, "a person *can* end up in somebody's arms without it meaning anything." Louisa followed her into the bedroom. "It meant nothing when you barged in on me and Clark. . .just like it meant nothing when you kissed that man."

Meera knew Louisa was being facetious, making her point by saying the opposite of what she really meant. At least, Louisa didn't know who "that man" was. She only knew she'd seen him on Maxwell property.

"Who was he?" Louisa asked then.

"That's irrelevant!" Meera snapped. "John Doe—Sam Smith—a rose is a rose is a rose!" She threw a suitcase on the bed, opened it, and began taking out her clothes.

"Not if it smells like a *Maxwell*!" Louisa retorted.

Meera slammed the suitcase and shoved it in the closet. "I don't have to answer to you, Louisa."

"True." Louisa perched on the bed and crossed her long legs, looking very pleased with herself. "I'm sure Clark will understand."

Meera drew in a deep breath before she closed the closet door and turned to face her cousin. "I'm not so sure, Louisa. I don't think Clark will understand at all. He seems to have a double standard when it comes to men and women."

119

Louisa shrugged. "He just knows what he wants in a relationship, and frankly, Meera, I think you're too independent to fit the bill."

"But *he* proposed to *me*, Louisa," Meera shot back.

Louisa picked at the chenille bedspread. "I think you'd both be making a big mistake."

Meera resented the turmoil in her life, for which she'd blamed Clark and Louisa, ignoring the fact that she'd felt a burden drop from her shoulders when she took off the engagement ring. Nevertheless, her heart went out to her cousin whose downcast face and trembly lips said much more than her words. Louisa was in love with Clark—and Meera could understand her frustration.

"Look, Louisa," she said softly, "I don't want to fight with you or Clark or anyone anymore, including the Maxwells."

Louisa's head came up, her eyes wide. "You told him about the property?"

"Not yet. But I intend to."

Louisa shook her head, disbelieving.

"I might as well tell you. The family will have to know." Meera slumped down into an easy chair. "I went to Chestnut Lodge under the name Meera Brown so I could study the Maxwells and decide for myself if they were worthy to be informed about the property sale."

"And were they?" Louisa prompted.

"I only met. . .one," Meera confessed, her voice trailing off. "He's. . .just like us, Louisa. A human being who's been raised to hate the name of Briskin, like we hate the name of Maxwell. But he's fair, and decent, and. . ."

"You let a Maxwell kiss you!?" Louisa screeched, jumping from the bed and placing her hands on her hips.

"Oh, cut the threatrics, Louisa."

But Louisa stood her ground, nodding accusingly.

"He thought I was Meera Brown. He—he liked me, and I couldn't be too resistant or I couldn't get to know him, and my purpose there would be defeated."

"And now that you've accomplished your purpose, does it mean that you're going back to Venezuela with us?"

"I have some thinking to do first. Anyway," Meera continued gravely, "the family might disown me after they find out what I've done and. . .what I intend to do."

"Who's going to tell them?"

Meera drew in an exasperated breath. "Well, believe me, Louisa, I'm going to try to beat you to it."

Seeing her cousin's crestfallen expression, Meera was immediately contrite. She'd tried not to strike out at Louisa, who had been reared as a spoiled, only child, accustomed to getting whatever she wanted. What could she expect? "I'm sorry."

"I guess I deserved that," Louisa said humbly, much to Meera's surprise. "I've already done a lot of thinking." She turned a mischievous grin. "Didn't know I could, did you, Cuz?"

"I didn't know you *would*!"

"Well, I've made a decision," Louisa announced and, seeing that Meera wasn't going to ask, she added. "I'm not going to Venezuela until you do."

Meera gave her a skeptical glance, then began to unpack the cosmetic case and place the items on the dresser top.

"I mean it. I'm going to back you in this Maxwell thing. I really don't care who buys my slice of that mountain. I just want the money. Also," she paused, waiting until she knew she had Meera's full attention, "I'm not going to try to take Clark away from you."

Meera looked at her cousin's reflection in the mirror. "You already tried that."

"Not very hard," Louisa contradicted her.

Meera grimaced. In that case, Clark had succumbed to Louisa's charms with only the slightest provocation. "That's sweet of you, Louisa. But I want to be alone for a few days."

"Oh, I wouldn't stay here. I'll stay at the estate."

Meera shrugged. "That's your decision, but don't do it on my account. If you and Clark have something going between you, then I want to know it before I make a lifetime commitment to him."

"I'm staying," Louisa insisted. "I don't like this bickering between us. We're behaving like. . .like Briskins and Maxwells."

Meera gave her a sharp look, walked through the cabin, and banged the front screen behind her. She heard the gurgling creek, but refused to look on the other side. Instead, she dragged her clothes from the silver convertible and returned to the bedroom where she laid them across the bed.

"If you stay, Louisa," Meera began skeptically, "what's your real reason?"

Louisa gave her a searching look, then tossed her dark hair behind one shoulder. With much more candor than Meera would have given her credit for, she affirmed, "I want to find out how you intend to deal with that rose of yours. . .without getting stuck with the thorns."

❧

Thorns? No, not anymore, Meera decided. Elliot Maxwell had done her no harm, nor had any other member of his family. As far as she was concerned, the feud was over.

With that determination, she put the silver cup on the mantel, set herself a deadline, compiled all the notes she had taken while at Chestnut Lodge, laid out the information and photographs Elliot had given her, and proceeded to make an outline. Meera was delighted to discover that the article came together more quickly than articles she had written previously, and attributed it to the conference instruction and handouts.

It was past 2:00 A.M. when the excitement and motivation fueled by adrenaline were replaced by sheer exhaustion. Meera opened a window far enough to allow a stream of cool evening air to invade the bedroom.

Turning down the bedspread, blanket, and top sheet, she put out the light, removed her robe, and crawled into bed. Safe from prying eyes, Meera allowed herself the luxury of a good cry, telling herself that it was the memories of her beloved grandfather triggered by her first night in the cabin, nothing more.

With the pungent odor of the forest floor permeating the room and the babble of the brook in her ear, Meera gave herself over to the wave of nostalgia that swept over her. She'd never talk to her grandfather again, or see his face, or listen to his sage advice. But before she fell asleep, she heard herself say, "Grandfather, am I doing the right thing? Would you approve? You'd never disown me, would you? After all, the Bible does tell us to 'love our enemies.'"

Her face still damp with tears, Meera finally fell into a deep sleep and did not awaken until the bright morning sun crept through the window. She blinked her eyes open to greet the day. Outside, the sound of squirrels and other woodland creatures scampering about industriously stirred her to action.

Hearing a car drive up outside, she jumped out of bed and, throwing on a robe, hurried to the front window to peek out. It was Louisa! She was unloading several heavy grocery sacks from the back seat. Meera ran out to help her.

"Did you tell the family?" Meera asked dubiously, wondering whether to welcome her cousin or send her packing.

"You know I've always been loyal to you, Cuz," Louisa

pouted. "We've kept each other's secrets all our lives, haven't we? It's just that little one with Clark, and you're letting it ruin our friendship."

Meera sighed. It wouldn't do any good to say "that little one with Clark" was quite different from all the other secrets they had shared as children. "What is all this?" she wanted to know, tightening the sash of her robe and stepping carefully in her bare feet on the gravel drive.

"Didn't want you to starve to death, dear cousin."

Meera was touched. It was just like Louisa. Despite their past differences, they'd always made up. First, a quarrel. Then a peace offering. This time Meera was truly grateful. It would save her a trip to town for supplies.

"Thanks. Guess I was just shocked to see you up and around so early."

"Early?" Louisa scoffed and handed Meera a sack. "It's almost eleven o'clock."

"Oh, no," Meera moaned. "I've wasted half a day already."

Louisa cocked an inquisitive brow. "What do you have to do?"

"Oh, come on in," Meera said with a sigh of resignation. "I'll tell you over coffee."

"Oh," Louisa said, peering intently at the surrounding area, "someone was sneaking around over there across the creek the other night."

Meera refused to follow the direction of her cousin's gaze. Instead, she headed for the porch with the bag of groceries.

Louisa followed her in pursuit. "I saw a man. And you know what, Meera? I would swear he was the same one you made that 'mistake' with last night."

So that's why Louisa was here? To rub it in! Devious little cousin! "You're incorrigible, Louisa! You know that?"

Meera opened the screen door, balancing the sack. Louisa

stuck out her foot to hold the door open. "I'd say we're cut out of the same cloth, cousin," finished Louisa on a triumphant note.

"We'll see," Meera mused. Maybe her cousin was right. "We'll just see."

While the coffee perked, Meera showed her the layout for the article—pictures, recipes, outline, notes.

Over coffee and sweet rolls, Meera confided to Louisa that she'd decided to inform Elliot Maxwell of the impending sale of the property. "I don't like being part of some feud that I didn't start. I want it stopped. Do you, Louisa? Do you want to help me put a stop to this? I mean, if two of us approach the family. . ." She paused, noting the fear that leapt into Louisa's eyes. "Then again, maybe you and I aren't cut from the same cloth, after all."

Louisa picked at her sweet roll and poked a crumb into mouth. Then she looked over at Meera. "Well, we do tend to go after what we want. . .in spite of what the family might think."

Meera stared at her cousin. Was Louisa saying that she had deliberately gone after Clark, regardless of the pain it might cause anyone else? If the shoe had been on the other foot—if Louisa and Clark had been engaged—Meera would never have made a play for him. At least, she didn't think she would. But then, only last week, she would have sworn she'd never in her wildest dreams have found herself in the arms of a Maxwell. And *liking* it! She looked over at Louisa. "Then you'll help me?"

"As they say on the soaps," Louisa said, anticipation sparking her dark eyes, "try me."

If Meera couldn't trust her cousin with Clark, maybe she could trust her with this. It was worth a shot. Besides, it was inevitable that her family would find out anyhow, and she might as well start with Louisa.

Meera laid out the plan: Louisa would go to the Arboretum in Asheville to pick up some information on the chestnut blight. She would also bring a good typewriter from the big house. Meera herself would call the family and tell them that she would be at the cabin for a while, writing, but she'd get in touch with them next week, before returning to Venezuela.

Louisa's mouth dropped open. "You're going back. . .next week?"

"Of course. Does that surprise you?"

"Well, I thought you were so mad at Clark and me that you might never go back."

"I'm not mad anymore, Louisa. But something as important as a marriage proposal requires a face-to-face confrontation, don't you think?"

Louisa glanced over at Meera's hand, resting on the table. "But you're still not wearing his ring."

Self-consciously, Meera put her hand in her lap. "It's what's in my heart that counts, Louisa, not what's on my finger. But if it makes you happy. . ."

She retrieved the ring from an inner zippered compartment of her purse and put it on. It felt heavy. . .like a rock. But now maybe Louisa would hush.

Unpredictably, her cousin was silent, though her face clouded over.

Meera began clearing the table. "I have more room on this big table. I think I'll put the typewriter in here."

Louisa accurately took that as a dismissal. "Anything else I can do?"

"You could get our airline tickets."

There was a glint of rebellion in Louisa's dark eyes. "What day did you have in mind?"

"End of next week. Um, Friday, I think. I should wrap up

my business here by then."

"You're not going to tell him who you are?"

Meera walked over to the sink and set the coffee cups down. "I can't," she said sorrowfully, looking out the window at the towering mountainpeaks beyond.

"You can't?" Louisa repeated.

"Not yet. Not until after he approves the article. Sees that I mean no harm."

This scenario was beginning to unfold like one of Louisa's favorite soaps. "Then. . .when will you tell him?"

"I'm not sure I will," Meera replied. "I might just have the attorney inform him of the sale and stay out of it myself."

It was a long moment before Louisa spoke again. "I'd better go, but I dread it. Mom and Dad are not going to understand why I'm waiting till next week to return to Venezuela. I'll just tell them you need me here. So. . .you know where you can find me. I'll be at the big house."

Meera turned to face her cousin. "After all I gave you to do in town?"

"Oh, I mean I'll be at the house when I'm not running around playing secretary," Louisa said with a toss of her dark hair. "I guess you know this is going to cost you."

Meera smiled. She didn't doubt that for a minute. Louisa's favors were few and far between, and she apparently hoped there might be something in this for her.

***

Forgetting Meera was as difficult as Elliot had imagined it would be. She had made him remember Kate. . .then she had made him forget Kate and put her in her proper place with bittersweet memories. But the beautiful blonde with soft gray eyes was an image forever engraved on his mind. Her warmth, her caring, her sweet passionate kisses had created a turmoil inside that he couldn't shake.

The matter wasn't really ended—he knew that—and he was eager to know what the outcome would be. Would she finish the article, then tell him who she really was? Or did she intend to have it published, thinking he'd never know the author was really Meera Briskin? Was it some kind of joke that she and the dark-haired woman were playing on him?

No. There would be a confrontation of some kind—at some time. However, he didn't feel it was his place to contact her. She had started this, and she should be the one to pursue it toward whatever end she had in mind.

Putting the troubling thoughts aside, Elliot busied himself with the never-ending work at the lodge. Although the peak season began in mid-June, spring was more demanding in many ways for the full-time staff. It was a favorite time for many tourists. And when there were no guests to deal with directly, there was always paperwork, inventory, ordering, maintenance. He tackled the applications for summer staffers and made his decisions within two days. Also, there was correspondence from former guests who had known his dad for years and wanted the latest update on his condition.

But despite the busyness, Elliot could not stave off the memories of Meera for long. Even before Josh had mentioned it, Elliot had realized he was falling for her, but didn't want to face the complications of loving a Briskin. But he could no longer dismiss the reality. It was a problem they must resolve. . .together.

Maybe she was frightened of him. Maybe she was wise to wait until emotions had cooled. But she would contact him again. He was sure of it. . .well, almost sure.

He lunched with Trevor at a small restaurant in the valley. They talked of mutual friends, books they had read and enjoyed, world events, and future goals, which served as a welcome diversion from his roiling thoughts. The subject of Meera didn't come up, and Elliot was relieved, though he knew Trevor rarely discussed his own private life.

Late at night, when the sky had turned to a velvet showcase of starry diamonds, Elliot found himself lonelier than he had ever been. Since there was nothing pressing at the lodge, he tried reading a book Trevor had suggested. But he couldn't concentrate. Instead, he swam in the pool, his eyes wandering frequently to the third-floor balcony.

Perhaps he should go to the cabin to be sure she was all right. But he knew a Briskin would be as adept at survival in the forest as a Maxwell. She would have grown up with guns and rifles. Besides, the hunting lodge would be equipped with modern means of reaching help if needed. In any event, the same security officers who patrolled Maxwell property also patrolled Briskin property, to protect against trespassers and poachers, but more importantly, to report the first ominous sign of a forest fire.

Due to his grim mood, even the staff had stopped asking about the article and if he were still talking to the attractive writer about it or knew when it would be published.

"These things take time," he would snap, so they now took pains to stay out of his way.

Elliot's mom called to remind him that he hadn't been by the house in days and asked solicitously if he were working too hard.

"I have been," he said with sudden clarity, realizing he wasn't handling this whole thing very well. "But I'm taking the rest of the afternoon and evening off, so I'll drop by."

"Then come for supper, dear," she encouraged. "I'm having your favorite stew."

Over dinner, his mother, who could read him like a book, grilled him. "What's bothering you, Elliot?"

Rather than shrug aside her question, he answered honestly.

"Just something I have to work out by myself, Mom."

His dad observed him over his bifocals. "I've found, son, that when we're troubled, it's usually not because we don't know what to do, but because we don't want to do it."

"Dad, it's not that simple," Elliot protested.

"Didn't say it was." Max Maxwell picked up his fork and dug into his apple cobbler.

For the rest of the meal, there was little conversation. Elliot thought back to his younger years and the "problem" that had existed for as long as he could remember. His parents and grandparents had instilled in him a respect for the forest and its wildlife, as well as survival techniques for coping with its dangers. When he was thirteen, his dad and granddad had deemed it time for him to accompany them and a few of their hired hands to the forest. They taught him how to spot trees that were to be cut—which should be cleared and which should be left—and when new saplings should be planted.

He had worked alongside the adults all that summer and fall, feeling the tug of growing muscle and flesh and the still, small voice within as he communicated with the God who had created the wilderness.

Then in the winter of his fourteenth year, his grandfather had died. Being the only grandchild, Elliot had been showered with love and attention, and the pain of losing his grandfather had been severe. Growing up was tough.

In the spring of his fifteenth year, his dad had taken him for a walk through the woods, to show him where they intended to clear away some of the forest near the creek, so that it might serve as a natural fire break. Elliot had welcomed that time of hard work to keep his mind off the loss of his grandfather, and his closeness with his dad deepened. As the work progressed and they moved farther up the property line, they saw that workers on the Briskin side of the creek had similar ideas and were building a road.

It was a hot day, and the Briskin help were burning a big pile of rubble near the creek that curved sharply into Maxwell property. Here, because of the topography of the land, the line was indistinct, though it was soon apparent that Max Maxwell was sure his sworn enemies were too close for comfort.

Elliot saw a muscle flex in his dad's jaw. "It might be a good idea to burn that stuff a little closer to the creek," he called to the workers.

A silver head lifted, and Elliot knew from the anger that washed over his face that he was not just an employee but one of the Briskins themselves. "I think we're capable of handling this. . .without any help from a Maxwell," he said stiffly.

"Apparently not," Max snorted, "or you wouldn't be burning so close to our thickest stand of trees! One little spark can send these mountains up in smoke in a matter of minutes."

"Look here," Briskin ordered, "keep your nose out of our business, and we'll all be just fine!"

Elliot's dad bristled. "If you destroy one leaf on my property, you'll wish you'd never seen a forest!"

Briskin laughed derisively as his boots splashed into the creek on his way over to the Maxwell side. "And just what are you planning to do about it? Shoot me like your ol' man shot my dad? I won't be the one to run away limping, I can tell you that!"

Elliot had reached out to take his dad's arm, but his father had shrugged him away. Workers on both sides glared at each other, ready to defend their respective employers.

The two men fired a volley of accusations and denials that turned the air blue, taking the quarrel back to their own fathers and the chestnut blight. Their tempers flamed hotter than the burning rubble, and Elliot's dad stepped over into the creek himself, onto Briskin property. They began shoving each other, while their language grew ugly and vicious.

The shoving turned into a flurry of punches, fists striking at whatever portion of the anatomy presented itself—knuckle on cheekbone, chest, gut. At last they both tumbled into the creek, wallowing like pigs in a hog trough.

Before he knew it, Elliot was in the creek, pulling on the Briskin man and crying like a baby. "Stop it! Leave my dad alone!"

At this point the workers got into the fray, pulled the men apart and led them, dripping, from the creek.

"What kind of man are you anyway, fighting in front of your own kid like that?" Briskin growled.

"The kind that will protect his heritage from the likes of you!" Max shot back. "We lost enough because of Briskin, and it won't happen again! Like I said, if a single leaf on one of my trees is destroyed, you'll answer to me personally, and I won't be as kind as my dad. . .I won't shoot for the knees!"

"Don't threaten me, Maxwell. You think I'm not ready for you?" Briskin snorted and glanced around at his own men. "You can't reason with a low-down so and so like that. Put the fire out. He's not worth wasting our time on. You can see he doesn't even care about what he's doing to his own kid."

"My dad's not. . ." Elliot yelled, but Max stopped him with a look.

"No, son, not a word." Shrugging out of the grasp of his men, Max came over and put his arm around Elliot's shoulder. "Let's go home."

And when Elliot glanced back, he saw the Briskin workers getting a pump from the back of a pickup truck, apparently either planning to douse the fire or to be ready in case of an errant spark.

Elliot didn't feel like a man that day, but a helpless child.

He'd been warned all his life about the Briskins, but this was the first time he'd seen the animosity in action, and it was a fearful thing that had possessed his dad like a fever. It had also shown Elliot how unreasonable the Briskins could be, how dangerous, and how easily a good man could lose his cool when provoked.

His dad had talked to him for a long time that day, reinforcing what Elliot had been taught all his life—that Briskins were conniving cheats and not to be trusted. Elliot knew his dad was not a violent sort, so he blamed the Briskins. And thereafter, rather than risk facing one of them, he deliberately took the long way around the creek.

Now Elliot thought of something his dad had said recently: "It isn't that we don't know what to do, it's that we don't want to do it." Looking back, he wondered if his father might have been referring to that incident. Could it be that he knew he had been in the wrong, but wasn't willing to make amends? Wouldn't he like to make it right now?

Maybe I need to do something, Elliot debated with himself. Meera had taken the first step. At least, she had crossed the boundary. Had dared to set foot on Maxwell property. And after the fiasco with the dark-haired woman who had been spotted on Briskin property, Meera knew that he knew she was somehow connected to the Briskins.

Is it time to take some initiative of my own? Elliot mused. Were Meera a man, it might be a different matter. But he wasn't at all concerned that he would be tempted to fight with Meera Briskin.

By Thursday night and still no word from Meera, he decided to go to the cabin and confront her. He'd be reasonable. Simply ask a few questions. Let her know she had no reason to fear him. On a couple of occasions, he felt sure she had been about to tell him who she was. He could stop behaving like a kid playing games and make it easier for her.

With that resolve, he become more and more fidgety as the day wore on. And right after supper, he knew he needed to get it over with.

When he reached the creek, he was shocked to find that her car was gone. Darkness had come early, but no lights appeared in the windows. The cabin was apparently empty.

He stood near the rocks, feeling foolish and as helpless as the day he'd seen their dads fighting. Then it dawned on him. Why should Meera be living in that little cabin when she had access to the Briskin estate and her parents' home in Charlotte? Well, this little escapade had backfired on him. With his hands in his pockets and his eyes on the ground, he followed the path beside the creek, seeing white dogwood petals—like so many butterflies—floating on the light breeze.

Ignoring the distant rumblings of the heavens and thick gray clouds rolling in, he shuffled on. Too late he realized that the spring storm was more severe and closer than he had imagined, and the cold pellets of rain that struck his face sharply came as a surprise.

He turned around and hurried back up the creek. When he glanced toward the cabin once more, he saw the front of the silver convertible and a light glowing against a window. His heartbeat quickened. She was home! Had she hidden the car out back in case he returned to the scene of their little rendezvous? Maybe she was afraid to let him know she was there, afraid of his reaction. After all, he had said some pretty nasty things about her family.

With that thought, he moved toward the lodge. But the jarring rumble raised the hair on the back of his neck, and he knew that lightning was about to strike. Making a beeline for the rocks, he crouched low against them as streaks sizzled through the sky.

It didn't take a mountain man to know that the worst place to be during a storm was under a tree, and there was nothing but trees all the way back up Maxwell Mountain. He could stay here, huddled close to the rocks and hope for nothing more than a light case of pneumonia. Or. . .he could do something *really* dangerous. He could see if Meera would take him in.

He had never set foot on Briskin land before, but he decided that he'd rather risk the wrath of a Briskin than stay here and be struck by lightning. After all, she had been the first to trespass, he reminded himself as the lightning flashed a warning, making the cabin dance in the forbidding darkness.

He took a deep breath, stood to his feet, and made a run for it straight through Turkey Creek. With a sudden downpour soaking his clothes clear to the skin, he hopped from rock to rock, losing his footing and getting a shoeful of icy water. Running across the lawn, he bounded up onto the porch, under the shelter of the overhanging roof. Then while the jagged streaks split the night sky, he jerked open the screen door and pounded furiously.

ten

Meera pecked away at the typewriter while the rain poured, tapping on the tin roof in time to the rhythm of her keys. Outside, the wind howled, lightning flashed in brilliant bursts, and thunder rattled the windowpanes. Although familiar with sudden spring thunderstorms, she was slightly annoyed with the distraction.

When she was little, her grandfather had told her that the rumble of a storm was no more threatening than a growling bobcat. It simply wanted to assert its authority and establish its territory.

Resolved to assert her own authority over the storm's intrusion, Meera smiled at the typewritten pages, pleased that this new project was developing so well. Last night, the final draft of the Chestnut Lodge article had been finished. Today, she'd researched the new one until mid-afternoon, then she'd napped.

After that, Meera had hiked up the mountainside behind the cabin and looked over at Chestnut Lodge. It was no longer the mystery it had been for twenty-four years. She'd met a Maxwell and had felt his arms around her. Did he wonder why she hadn't gone to his suite that night? Did he even care? Had he guessed that she was a Briskin? Did he hate her now?

After a sudden chilling wind had blown up, she had hiked back down the mountain, tempted to fish the stream for trout. But fearing Elliot might come down that way and see her, she'd hurried back to the cabin. She couldn't face him yet—maybe never. She'd showered, slipped on a pair of coral cotton-knit shorts and matching tank top, then had sat on the back porch with her sandaled feet propped on the only step. Her meager supper had consisted of a piece of cold fried chicken, followed by a yellow mountain apple. Then she'd stretched, reveling in the feeling of isolated freedom and the sense of security the surrounding mountains presented.

It was inevitable that she do some thinking. There were questions that must be answered. Did she want to tackle the ecological issues here on Briskin land, or become a bridge-playing, charity-ball-going Venezuelan socialite married to a man who could be tempted by the likes of Louisa? Or was she herself even ready for marriage—having been tempted by a. . . Maxwell?!

As twilight stole through the woods, she returned to the kitchen table with a cup of hot tea sweetened with honey and tackled the second writing project with renewed vigor, working all evening. She had almost finished when the wind began banging the front screen as if trying to rip it off its hinges. She'd better secure it.

Meera reached for the door just as lightning lit the sky, revealing a hulking figure holding the screen door open while she tried to close it. Startled, she jumped back and grabbed the rifle standing in the corner behind the door that was there for such an emergency. She had just swung it around to aim at the intruder when a loud voice boomed, "Hey! Hold it! I'm leaving."

"Elliot!" she gasped. "Is that you? I thought it was the wind! Or a black bear or something. What are you doing out there?"

"I'm either going to drown or become a lightning rod if I stand here much longer," he yelled above the storm. "But I suppose getting shot couldn't be much worse. After all, I *am* a trespasser."

As if to punctuate his remarks, another bolt of electricity

split the sky, bathing them both in the neon flash. They stood staring at each other for a second longer before Meera lowered the rifle and stepped back. "You'd. . .better come in," she said, while all sorts of tangled emotions tore through her.

She switched on the living room light, and he moved inside, shaking himself like a wet puppy. Meera closed the door and replaced the rifle in the corner. "I didn't think you'd ever set foot on Briskin property. What possessed you to do it?"

"Basic self-preservation. I'm trying to save myself from the storm. The question is. . .what are *you* doing here, Meera Brown?" he asked, as if he didn't know, telling himself that he was giving her one more chance to tell him the truth. "Did you get caught in the storm too? Or did that wild dark-haired woman kidnap you?" He glanced around as if half expecting her to appear.

She ignored his question. "I'm alone. Would you like to—to sit down?"

"Do you think we could be completely honest with each other now?" he asked, sounding as forlorn as he looked with water puddling at his feet.

Meera's heart lurched crazily. "Oh, I want that, Elliot! I really do!"

He stared at her for a long moment, touched by the uncertainty in her eyes and the contrition in her voice as she added, "And I hope you won't be angry with me."

That reasonable tone of voice sounded a note of alarm. "Should I be?"

"No, Elliot. Not if you hear me out." Her thin reply was almost drowned out by the pounding of the rain that whipped the house and slammed against the windows. Outside, the usually benign creek surged outside its banks like a wild thing and thunder shook the cabin. Suddenly the lights flickered and went out, plunging them into pitch-black darkness.

Elliot did not feel any compulsion to make her feel ill at ease or play any games as he'd intended the night before. Instead, by the intermittent light flashes outside the window, he could see her soft tremulous lips, the hesitancy in her eyes, and wanted more than anything to take her in his arms and reassure her.

"There's a flashlight in the desk drawer," she told him, but did not move to find it. Instead, she remained where she was, finding it curious that he was here, willing to talk, willing to listen. She fought a fierce desire to be cradled in his arms when she made her confession, but dared not risk rejection.

A sudden loud sneeze punctuated the silence, and Meera was jolted out of her reverie. "You're going to catch your death of cold, Elliot. You'd better get out of those wet things . . .your shirt, at least."

She gestured toward a low stool near the hearth, and he stumbled toward it, guided by the flashes of light outside the window.

Feeling some of the tension ease, he joked, "Socks too?"

She attempted a feeble laugh. "Sure. I'll look for the flash-light."

Making her way to the desk, Meera fumbled through a drawer until she found it. Then she turned it on and followed the yellow circle of light to the couch where she lifted her grandfather's afghan from the back. Turning, she captured Elliot in the beam. Squinting, he put up his hands and she quickly lowered the flash to his bare chest.

"Here, wrap up in this." She handed him the afghan and set the flashlight down beside him.

Elliot draped the wrap around his shoulders, grasping it with one hand. She was so close that he could smell the scent of her freshly shampooed hair, could almost feel the warmth of her. "Does the storm frighten you?" he asked softly.

"No," she said in a small voice, noting how the occasional bursts of light outside the window outlined his solid frame. But when a crash of thunder sounded, nearer than before, she instinctively reached for him, taking comfort in the strength of his muscular forearm beneath the soft wool wrap.

Unexpectedly, the lights came on again. Meera blushed, her hand still on his arm, her body nestled close to his. Then, too late, she realized that he was staring down at her hand. . . her *left* hand!

Elliot was stone cold—as cold as the wet breeches clinging to his legs. His gaze was locked on the hard object that glittered like cold fire on her finger. "Well, I see you've made your decision," he said blandly, his unemotional tone belying the ache in his heart.

"No. . .you don't understand," she choked out. "I mean. . ."

In the face of his shriveling disapproval, she stepped away. Feeling suddenly hot, the scratchy afghan prickling his skin, Elliot undraped himself. He was reaching over to lay the afghan in the recliner when he noticed an official-looking envelope on the end table.

"International Airlines." The cold steel of his voice sent a chill through Meera. "Somebody going away?"

"Oh, please. . .don't," she pleaded, but he had already picked up the open envelope, its contents protruding.

"Meera Briskin," he read. "Now who might *that* be? Leaving tomorrow. No," he corrected coldly, "leaving *today*." He tossed the envelope and ticket back onto the table.

She thought his eyes raking her as if she were a—a *Briskin*. She felt dirty. . .untouchable. "Please, Elliot, let me explain."

"Explain?" In two strides he reached the hearth, pausing long enough to hurl an accusation. "What's to explain. Isn't it quite obvious. . .Meera *Briskin*?"

He plunked himself down on the edge of the hearth and

forced his feet into wet shoes, then stood and stuffed his socks into his pants pockets. "And just for the record, I've known who you were since the first day you arrived at Chestnut Lodge."

Meera gasped. "You knew? And you've been pretending all this time?" Realizing the irony of her question, she dropped her eyes.

"No! *Waiting*. . .to see if you'd be honest with me. But, of course, that's a lot to ask of a Briskin! Be sure you include that part when you joke about your little deception with your dark-haired friend and your boyfriend—or husband—in Venezuela."

Meera stepped closer and touched his arm. "I'm not married."

Elliot shrugged her away as he reached for his shirt. "What's the difference? We both played our little games. Now it's over. That's all. But I can't see that anybody won." With difficulty, he wriggled into his wet knit shirt, then strode to the door. "I can't get out of here fast enough."

He held onto the doorknob, pausing long enough to deliver one last barb. "I know the article was some kind of ploy. I don't even want to know what kind. But just in case you have anything else in mind, let me make this clear. There is to be no article. If you try to publish one word, I'll sue!"

"Please, Elliot, you don't understand!" But he jerked the door open, oblivious to her desperation and the raging elements, and with a slam of the screen, he was gone.

The jarring sound was like the rumble through the heavens, as if Someone had tried to warn her. Her grandfather had been right—a Maxwell wouldn't listen to anything a Briskin had to say. And if Elliot had known her identity all along, then his emotional response to her had been. . .an act!

She closed the door and leaned back against it. The lights

went out again, leaving the room dark except for a red circle where the flashlight still shone on the hearth. After switching it off, Meera sat on the cold, damp stone, hugging her arms to her body.

Her good intentions had turned out to be nothing but ashes. *So what,* she said to herself, *if some developer builds condos all across the top of the mountain? I won't be here to see it. I'll go to Venezuela and to Clark—where I belong.*

ed

All morning, Elliot worked like a bear getting ready to hibernate. During the long night he had vowed to himself that he would never trust another woman as long as he lived, mentally kicking himself in the seat of the pants for letting himself get caught up in a Briskin scheme.

He couldn't believe he had been in the Briskin cabin, halfdressed. What a laugh the Briskins would have about that! Or they might not consider it a laughing matter. He'd never made such a fool of himself in his entire life. And the rotten thing about it was, he'd walked into it with his eyes wide open.

His intercom buzzed and the morning clerk broke into his train of thought. "Mr. Maxwell?"

Elliot growled into the phone, "I thought I told you to direct everything to the manager. If she can't handle it, then we don't need her."

"But she says it's a matter of life and death."

"She who?"

"Um. . .the young woman."

"Young woman!" he muttered under his breath. "Tell her I'm. . .out of town!"

"She says she knows you're here and she's not leaving until you see her, sir."

Elliot leaned back against the cool leather chair back and

closed his eyes. How much more did he have to take? "Is she a blonde?"

"Blonde?"

"You know. . .hair color!" he yelled. "Does she have blond hair?"

"No, sir."

Elliot threw down his pencil and stared at the door until it burst open. In charged the dark-haired hellion he'd encountered for the past two nights. He punched the intercom. "Get security in here," he demanded.

The woman marched up to the desk, gave him a scathing look, and threatened, "You call security, and I'll yell 'Fire!' to the top of my lungs!" And with that, she threw a manila envelope on his desk. "Now shall I start screaming?"

"Just say what you have to say, and then get out," he snapped, not doubting for a moment that she'd do it. . .and enjoy the process.

He punched the intercom. "Forget security. Everything's okay in here."

"You're sure, sir?"

Elliot hesitated. He wasn't at all sure. "It might be a good idea to pass by my door occasionally."

She grinned while Elliot got up and propped the door wide open.

"I'm Louisa Coleman," she said, putting out her hand. "Meera's cousin."

"You people have your nerve," he spat, ignoring her hand and returning to his chair behind the desk, hoping to put as much distance as possible between them.

"I'm also her friend."

"Well, as the saying goes, 'With friends like you, who needs enemies?'" he growled. "You're the one who tried to steal her fiancé, aren't you?"

"She told you that?" Louisa said, disbelievingly. Then after a moment, she shrugged. "Well, Meera doesn't know how to treat a man. She's kept poor Clark dangling all this time. It's no wonder he came on to me." She grinned again. "You can understand that, can't you?"

He wouldn't give her the satisfaction of hearing what he had on his mind at the moment. "Sounds like you and poor Clark are two of a kind," he said simply.

"I quite agree." Louisa lifted her chin defiantly. Then her mood changed and she purred, "And what kind are *you*, Mr. Maxwell?"

He could have laughed. "What difference does it make?"

"A lot." She got out of the chair and sauntered over to the desk, leaned across and rested her chin on her elbow. Then with her red lips pursed prettily, she challenged him. "I think you and I could have a lot of fun. I'm not nearly as stuffy as my older, but more naive, cousin."

"You come any closer," Elliot snapped, "and I'll be the one to yell 'Fire.'"

Her eyes narrowed. "Just testing you, Mr. Maxwell."

He got up and, against his better judgment, turned his back on her to look out the window. "Why do you two feel you have to test me? Why can't you just leave me alone?" he asked dejectedly. He'd had enough. Too much.

"Meera's reasons are in that envelope. Mine are more. . . creative, shall we say. But you needn't worry. We're both leaving for Venezuela tomorrow morning. That is, *if* you read what's in that envelope." Her voice took on a threatening tone again. "I'm not going anywhere until you do."

Leaving tomorrow morning? Good riddance! He whirled around, sat down, and tore open the envelope.

"She sent you with this, huh?" he asked, taking the papers out.

"Oh, no! Meera would kill me if she knew I was here. You can't imagine what I went through just to get her to say I could mail it."

"Sure," he retorted sarcastically. "You look like you've been through the wringer, all right."

She giggled. "Why, Mr. Maxwell, I do believe you almost paid me a compliment."

He smiled wryly. "Some of the most beautiful flowers are among the most deadly."

Louisa cocked her head and studied him. "What did my cousin do to you?"

He couldn't very well say that Meera had deceived him, since he'd known who she was almost from the beginning. And he wasn't about to tell Louisa the real truth—that her cousin had trespassed on his property and stolen his heart. "I don't want to discuss her!" he muttered and began reading the article.

"This comes as no surprise," he said when he had finished. "It compares with other articles she's written. It's well done, but I don't want a Briskin publishing an article on anything about the Maxwells. And that's final!"

"Read the other one," she urged.

Elliot sighed but picked up the other paper-clipped stack of papers. When he was well into it, he swiveled around, his back to Louisa.

He read Meera's well-documented account of the chestnut blight and how it had destroyed the country's most valuable hardwood tree. He already knew that, quite well! But he had not known the Briskin version of the feud.

She outlined it in an objective way, reporting what Elliot had told her. Then she gave a moving rendition of Elias Briskin, not the monster he'd always imagined, but a great man, a fine man, whose heart and life had been broken by a

Maxwell.

It was an account of the blight upon two families, infected by the parasite of misunderstanding and unforgiveness. Her version was something to think about. But it didn't change anything.

He turned around and faced Louisa again. "I've finished. You can leave now."

"One more thing," she said and took a white envelope from her bag and held it out to him.

Elliot looked at the letterhead, imprinted with the name of a prestigious law firm. He recognized the name of the attorney. *What now?* Was he being sued for trespassing last night? Or worse—had Meera recorded his late-night foray with a hidden camera so she could blackmail him? He felt sick to his stomach and sweat beaded his forehead. How could he ever explain his way out of that fiasco—wearing an afghan and little else in the middle of the night at the Briskin cabin?

Slowly, he opened the envelope. It stated simply, clearly that the Briskin mountain adjacent to Maxwell property was expected to be placed in the hands of a realtor in the near future and that Meera Briskin wanted the Maxwells to be so informed.

Elliot bristled. "What's this all about? You expect me to believe that a Briskin would sell to a Maxwell? The last time that happened, the Maxwells were ruined and a Briskin got shot."

"It's Meera's idea," Louisa said defensively. "A developer is interested in that land. Meera wanted to be fair. She's that way." She rolled her eyes toward the ceiling. "She convinced me to go along with her, and my mama and daddy will do what I ask. The other relatives don't really care that much, so it's just Uncle George and Aunt Clara and Meera's parents to convince, but you're already informed so I think you may have a legal right even if some of them say no."

"I don't intend to do battle with any more Briskins," he said, tossing the letter aside. This had to be some kind of sinister scheme. These two cousins playing some kind of sick game. He rose. "If that's all, Miss Coleman, I have work to do."

Louisa got to her feet. "Just one more thing," she said and walked over to him, standing so close that he caught a whiff of her heady perfume. "You're really not bad for a Maxwell, you know. And I'm a Coleman, not a Briskin. Couldn't we forget that silly ol' feud and get better acquainted?"

Elliot put up both hands and backed away. "No offense, ma'am, but I'm not interested."

"I didn't think you would be," she said lightly. "I should be used to it by now. The only time a man spurns me is when Meera gets to him first."

Elliot stiffened. Maybe he'd move to Hawaii. Trevor had had the right idea at one point in his life. "Look," he said between gritted teeth, "I'm not falling for any more Briskin schemes."

"Amazing, isn't it, Mr. Maxwell," she said, eyeing him through narrowed lids, "what we fall for sometimes. . . . I'll leave now."

Louisa moved toward the door but halted in the doorway. "Meera says she's going to. . ." her voice broke, then she added, "to marry Clark. If you want her, you'd better stop her."

⋆

Stop her. . .stop her. . .stop her. . .if you want her. The words rang in Elliot's head for the rest of the afternoon. But it was not just a matter of what he wanted. He, Trevor, and Josh had talked many times about what *God* wanted for their lives. He felt a sudden burst of conviction. When was the last time he had consulted God in all this?

Now it was too late, he supposed, even for the Lord to intervene. Besides, he'd seen the ring on her finger. So. . .what was there to say? *Don't marry that rich playboy, Clark Phillips? Forget your family and I'll forget mine, and come away with me and live happily ever after?* Oh, it was no use.

Scuffing through the woods, he continued to hear the refrain. *Stop her. . .stop her. . .stop her.* It whispered through the trees on the wind. It laughed at him from the waters of the creek. Even the small forest animals seemed to be repeating its message, taunting him.

Later, back in his suite at the lodge, unable to rest, he rose from his bed while darkness still blanketed the hills and valleys outside, and wandered down to the chapel. The glow of the wall sconces in the hallway cast a triangle of light along the aisle that separated the shadowy benches. Faintly outlined against the back wall was a six-foot cross made of rugged chestnut beams.

He closed the door behind him, plunging the room into a chilling blackness, then quickly switched on a small lamp at the back. In the subdued light, the cross seemed to be beckoning and he moved nearer and sank down in one of the pews.

What am I supposed to do now, Lord? he prayed silently. He thought of Meera's grandfather, Elias Briskin, who had been in love with his grandmother, Carrie Spearman. Was Meera trying to get even for old Elias—trying to make a Maxwell fall in love with a Briskin—then break his heart?

He shook off the cloying thoughts. Whatever her motives, he loved her. He loved Meera Brown. . .who was also Meera Briskin. But she was like the elusive Christmas angel—

always just out of reach. And now he had lost her forever to a man who didn't deserve her. . .any more than *he* did!

The revelation was startling. Since when was he himself a paragon of virtue? *I'm no saint,* he thought ruefully. And in the darkened chapel, alone with God, Elliot Maxwell repented. "Lord," he prayed, "I'm sorry. I've been a disappointment to You in this situation. I haven't asked You for Your input. You know I want that girl. But if I can't have what I want, help me to want what is best for me, and for her. Give me the integrity to face up to it. Lord, I understand that this is not just a matter of two people—me and Meera—but two families who need to be reconciled. Although I'd like to make a deal, I'll try not to put conditions on my serving You. . .but I don't mind admitting it would be easier if I could have her by my side."

When Elliot rose from his knees, he saw that morning had come, for a soft glow filtered in through the skylight to the center of the room. With his eyes on the shaft of light, Elliot walked through it, then returned to his room to get ready for whatever the day would demand of him.

He did not feel his burden lift. As he showered and dressed, he thought of Josh who had never found a girl intended just for him. Josh had told him that he'd met someone in Charleston whom he'd hoped was the one, but their first conversation had revealed that she was in love with someone else, so Josh contented himself with being her friend.

Trevor had loved a wonderful woman who had ultimately entered a convent, and he had—with integrity and maturity—channeled his emotions into his novels and speaking engagements.

But I, Elliot chided himself, *what have I done? I've behaved like a sophomoric fool.* Love, he remembered, is action—not just feeling. Love wants the best for the object of one's affection, even if the best is. . .someone else.

His mind accepted the truth of that statement, but his rebellious heart was not so receptive.

❧

Three days later, after careful investigation by the Maxwell attorney, Elliot discovered that a developer was indeed interested in Briskin property, although the property was not yet on the market.

Elliot told his parents that he'd learned of it from a Briskin who felt the Maxwells should know in case they got a chance to bid on it. The only drawback was a dogwood fungus, but that was a problem on Maxwell land too, and was currently being dealt with successfully.

To Elliot's surprise, his dad appreciated the information and delivered the startling statment that, although he'd never expected a Briskin to sell to a Maxwell, perhaps there was a Briskin with a trace of goodness in him.

"It's a 'she,' dad. Not a 'he,'" Elliot said quietly.

He told them what he knew about Meera Brown, who had come to the conference to pursue a career in writing. They remembered the lovely young woman who had won the award.

"I stand corrected," his dad said slowly after reading her articles. He glanced at his wife who lifted a quizzical brow. "Perhaps there's a Briskin with a trace of goodness in her."

"I never thought I'd hear you say a thing like that, Dad," Elliot replied.

"Well, that heart attack brought me close to death, son," his dad said seriously. "Before that, I felt I was invincible, immortal. Now I know how fragile life is. . .and how precious. Makes a man consider what's really important. . .like finding the right partner." He reached across the table and grasped his wife's hand. "And getting things squared away with the good Lord."

There wasn't much Elliot could do about finding a wife right now. The one he wanted was on her way to Venezuela to join the man she had promised to marry. But there was plenty he could do about his spiritual life. And he wouldn't waste another moment.

eleven

The summer season passed quickly for Elliot. By mid-June, the lodge was filled with guests and conferences that had been booked for months. Summer staffers were housed in their quarters near the lodge. And Elliot had made some headway in his quest for a closer relationship with God. He'd even spent more time than usual in the chapel where his breakthrough had occurred and in the woods, taking long solitary prayer walks.

Elliot had resigned himself to the probability that Meera had married Clark by now. He had only himself to blame for letting his emotions take precedence over his good sense. But then, he'd never felt this way about a woman before. His feelings for Kate had eventually been affected by the drugs that ravaged her personality. Still, he had seen the potential there and had begun to love the kind of woman Kate should have been. . .could have been. . . if!

Meera's obvious beauty, her warmth, her inner worth had been qualities he had admired from the beginning, far outweighing any fault he found in her. He had even begun to feel a kinship with Elias Briskin, who had lost the woman he loved to a Maxwell.

Remembering the fight between his father and Meera's, Elliot now realized that the two men had not been angry with each other—they had simply been victims of the feud that fed upon misunderstanding, always ready to break out. It was a spirit of discord that permeated both families. But because of Meera, he would never feel that way again, and he loved her for releasing him from that bondage.

He would tell her someday. . .maybe. . .if they ever met again. But during the summer, he stayed as far away as possible from the creek and any view of the cabin.

Then, one hot day in August, she called. "This is Meera. . . ." she said hesitantly.

"Hold on. . . ." He raced to another phone, hoping she wouldn't hang up on him. "Sorry, I wanted to take the call in my office."

"You're not going to believe this. . . ."

"Shoot!" he said, then laughed lightly. "Uh. . .please don't take me literally."

"I don't know how this happened," Meera continued apologetically, "but *Fabulous Places* magazine has a copy of my Chestnut Lodge article. They sent me a check. I swear I didn't submit it. . . ."

"*I* did."

"What?"

"It's a very good article. My dad gave his approval."

"Does he know who I am?"

"Yes," Elliot said. "Or at least he did. And who are you now, Meera? Brown, Briskin, or Phillips?" He caught his breath. "I'm sorry. I shouldn't have put you on the spot like that." His words came quickly then. "I wish you well."

"Thank you," she said, hating herself for feeling like she had static on the brain—static that seemed to be transferring to the telephone line. "The connection's going bad," she said, and closed her eyes against the pain that washed over her. As Meera Brown, she had connected so well with Elliot. But that was over now.

How long they listened to the crackle on the line, he didn't know. And when he spoke again, he wasn't sure how much she had caught of his message. "If they don't use a picture of

Bertha, I'm liable to lose a very good employee."

"I'll insist," she called over the crackle. "I'll bring. . .extra copies."

Bring, she had said, not *send.* "You're in the States?"

"Venezuela."

The line went dead and Elliot stared at the phone for a long time. A sense of abandonment like he hadn't felt since the last night he'd seen her, washed over him, shaking him and leaving him bent double like a sapling in a strong wind.

Apparently she had been in Venezuela all summer. She had intimated that Clark wanted a stronger commitment. Maybe the international playboy had actually married her. A person like Meera would not settle for less, he knew. He'd heard that love has the power to change people. Maybe it had changed Clark Phillips.

"Maybe someday I'll discover that my feelings for Meera were based on the game she and I were playing," Elliot told Josh when they talked later, "and the euphoria over the fact that a Maxwell and a Briskin were communicating."

"Do you really believe that, Elliot?"

Elliot shook his head. "No. . .I don't."

"It's easier for me to give advice than for you to take it, old pal, because I've never been in love. Oh, I've met women that I would like to have fallen in love with, even wished our relationship might grow into it. But it never happened. So, in my limited experience, I can only say: Trust the Lord to know what's best and to work things out according to His will."

Elliot grinned. "Yep, it's easier said than done. But I know you're right." He grew suddenly serious. "But I'm afraid the Lord has already decided there is to be no relationship between me and Meera. That is, Meera and Clark Phillips have decided."

"You can't reverse what's happened, Elliot," Josh reminded

him.

Elliot nodded. "And I can't force her to love me. All my attempts at relating have resulted in failure."

"Then wait on the Lord," Josh advised, "but stay busy."

❧

Elliot tried, but he was still in limbo. Maybe news would come that Meera had definitely married Clark, and he could begin to put her out of his mind. Or somehow his longing for her would subside. But nothing he did eased the ache deep within.

Then autumn came. The lush green of the mountains blazed in a rich tapestry of brilliant color, and the air turned crisp. The tourist season would end soon after the turning of the leaves.

When the cold, rainy season set in, the leaves lost their color and fell to the ground, leaving the limbs barren except for the evergreens that darkened to yet a deeper green. Then in mid-November, Indian summer came to the dun-colored hills and valleys. Autumn, punctuated by the blood-red leaves of the flame bush and fiery oranges and yellows of the marigolds in the flowerbeds around the lodge, seemed determined to go out in a blaze of glory.

Elliot took some comfort in this, his favorite season, and spent more time outside, involved in ecological activities in the forest. And for the second day in a row, he and his workers saw surveyors on Briskin property.

❧

During the second week in November, Meera returned to her parents' home in Charlotte. The family was planning to gather at the Briskin estate for the holidays and those who could, would arrive by Thanksgiving. Meera had research to do and interviews to conduct. *Fabulous Places* had scheduled an April date for the publication of her Chestnut Lodge article and assured her that they would use the picture of Bertha holding a dish of macaroon glacés. In addition, the editor wanted to see other articles in her proposed series on western North Carolina inns.

"I've called a surveyor, Meera," her father told her one morning just before Thanksgiving. "Your mother and I will be driving up to the estate tomorrow afternoon."

It couldn't be put off any longer. That night, Meera told her mom about the writers' conference, the article she had written on Chestnut Lodge, and her strategy to make peace with the Maxwell clan.

"I married into this family, Meera," she said dolefully. "And regardless of my private opinion about the feud, my place is to stick by my husband. You know that."

While telling her mother had been a breeze, telling her father was another matter. Meera weighed her words carefully. "I'm going to close the cabin for the winter," she told him early the next morning. "Will you go down with me?"

He was more than willing. "The surveyors are coming at nine A.M. I'll come by the cabin after I've shown them which piece of property we intend to sell."

Around noon, she served sandwiches and lemonade to the surveyors on the back porch and left the pitcher and glasses for seconds when they completed the job Mr. Briskin had outlined—to guarantee Meera access to the cabin from the main road as well as the back way down the mountain from the estate.

After lunch, while she cleaned out the refrigerator, her dad checked the pipes to make sure they were securely insulated for the winter. Seeing him straighten from his cramped position under the sink, Meera suggested, "Time for a break, Dad."

And with a quick prayer for guidance, she stepped into the living room, took her silver cup from the mantel, and brought it into the kitchen.

"What's that?" he wanted to know.

Meera sighed. "You'd better sit down."

Over coffee, Meera told him about her escapade at Chestnut Lodge, the article that would appear in April, and how she had inadvertently perpetuated the feud, causing at least one Maxwell—Elliot—to consider her devious and conniving.

Her dad was silent for a long time, pondering the gravity of what she had told him. Finally, he shook his head. "You say the fellow knew who you were, but pretended not to?"

Meera nodded.

He ran his hands through his silver hair. "It's just like I've always said, there's no reasoning with a Maxwell. Don't suppose you could expect any more than that from the son of Jonas Maxwell."

Meera stared at him. "Elliot is his *grand*son, Dad."

Now it was her father's turn to stare. "The boy?"

"Well, he's not exactly a boy."

"He was the last time I saw him," he said slowly, reminiscently. "I think Maxwell had only one. And the boy? He's not. . .married?"

She shook her head. "He loved someone who was murdered. Kate. . .Logan, I believe."

There was a moment while her dad pondered this latest information. Then, "Yes, I remember. It was several years ago. Made all the papers. Terrible tragedy for one so young and for those. . .left behind."

Meera closed her eyes, feeling the moisture trickle down her cheeks while he sat watching her. Then he took a handkerchief, leaned over, and blotted the tears. "You've been through a lot this past year, honey. We lost your granddad, then this noble venture of yours turned sour, then this thing with Clark. Do you think that's really over, baby?"

"Clark is not right for me, Dad. At least, not as a husband. He and Louisa are much better suited to each other."

"Well, all I know is that my beautiful girl should be happy," he said softly. "You seemed so happy with Clark. What happened, honey?"

Meera took the handkerchief from his hand and finished mopping up. "I *was* happy. . .for a while. But I guess I learned that happiness isn't all there is to life."

"Doesn't the Constitution say we're entitled to the pursuit of happiness?" he joked, hoping to make her laugh.

She obliged him with a watery smile. "Well, the Bible doesn't say anything about that. I think it talks about an *abundant* life, and that means more than just having a good time." She sobered and looked down at the damp handkerchief knotted in her hands. "I want my life to count for something."

Her father covered her hand with his large one. "Oh, honey, it does and it will. You have a terribly wonderful conscience and a warm heart. You just continue to pursue that abundant life, and it will be yours." He stood and looked down at her. "But I know this is a trying time for you. So, let's get that property on the market, forget the Maxwells, and get on with our lives. Now, how can I help you?"

For the next half hour they packed her grandfather's personal papers and pictures and put them in the car. Meera hoped to write a novel about the chestnut blight and the misunderstanding that had made bitter enemies of friends and destroyed what might have been a beautiful relationship between herself and Elliot. Someday. . .she'd write it.

It was mid-afternoon when they left the cabin and returned to the estate. Meera unpacked the box of memories and set the silver cup on her dresser. She would keep it always, just as her grandfather had kept letters and a diary of his early, happier days with the Maxwells and his memories of Carrie Spearman.

Yet, in spite of everything, her grandfather had lived an active, productive life. She would strive for that too.

It was almost dark when it sounded—like a jet breaking the sound barrier—yet somehow different. Suddenly a screaming wail sent a chill through her veins.

Meera bolted from the bedroom and ran down the two flights of stairs to the drawing room where her mother stood listening as her dad talked on the phone. It was the fire department.

Fire! It had to be the cabin.

⁊⋗

Elliot came in at sunset and went directly to his office. It was there he heard the loud boom. . .varoom. . .that seemed to shake the very foundation of the mountains, followed by a moment of silent panic.

Then came the shouting. "Fire!" "There's a fire in the forest!" "Down by the creek. . ." "Fire!"

The dreaded word ricocheted off the mountainsides and came over Elliot's voice pager. He pushed the intercom button to all offices. "Fire!" he shouted. "Sound the alarm!"

But Tom had already flipped the switch. Upon hearing the ear-splitting alert, guests began pouring into the lobby and spilled out onto the patio, peering into the forest to determine the source of the billowing smoke.

Elliot stood by the desk phone until the location of the fire was reported.

"It's the Briskin cabin, sir," said an employee. "Should we just keep the Maxwell side watered down?"

"Is anyone there?" he yelled.

"We don't know. Can't see a vehicle. Smoke's too thick."

"Sometimes they park at the back. Check it out."

"Sir, there was an explosion. It's. . .pretty far gone."

"Do what you can!" Elliot slammed down the receiver. "Call the fire department and report the fire at the Briskin cabin," he instructed his secretary on his way out. "Then tell Tom to break out the shovels and rakes and line up some people to help. I'm going down there."

He raced down the mountain at the back of the lodge, the tinder-dry leaves crunching beneath his feet. He could see the ominous glow—not the sunset painting the sky orange, but the glare of fire against the late evening sky. Clouds of gray smoke billowed above the trees. The pungent odor of burning pine needles and dry leaves mingled sharply with the cooler, crisp air, taking from it some of the oxygen and leaving behind a strong scent of woodsmoke.

When Elliot reached the creek, he saw that his men had driven Chestnut Lodge trucks across the creek onto Briskin property and were raking leaves into the clearing surrounding the cabin, while others were pumping water from the creek and hosing down the perimeter. They were helpless, however, to prevent the fire from racing up the mountain at the back of the cabin, for their hoses wouldn't reach that far.

Crossing over, Elliot felt his heart plummet to the pit of his stomach, seeing that the back of the cabin was in flames and part of the roof had already caved in. American chestnut wood was virtually fireproof and relatively smokeless, but the cabin had been standing for decades, and there had been an explosion. The cabin was burning steadily.

"We couldn't get inside, Mr. Maxwell!" someone called. "I don't think anyone was in it, but if they were, it's too late now!"

Too late! screamed through his head like the sirens coming on the scene, immediately followed by the fire engines, now lining up along the creek and the back road from the Briskin estate right behind a long black car that pulled to the side of the road to let them pass.

At this point, it was far more important to sacrifice the cabin, if necessary, than chance letting the fire spread, endangering thousands of acres of timberland. Since the firefighters were hard at work, however, Elliot directed his efforts to dousing the cabin. He had to save it for Meera, if possible. It meant so much to her.

Within minutes, the fire marshal had assessed the situation and praised Elliot and his staff for their prompt and professional action. He then directed the firefighters to move on up the mountain to build a firebreak above the fire. A staging area was set up on the Maxwell side of the creek with trucks, equipment, and an ambulance.

Several hours later, they had done all they could and now could only try to contain the fire. The terrain was too steep for bulldozers, and they could only hope the wind did not pick up and that the flames would not jump the firebreak. Additional workers arrived and went up the mountain with five-gallon tanks on their backs to put out any scattered fires. Others carried tools and equipment. Helicopters wouldn't be able to drop their barrels of water before morning.

Many of them, like Elliot, could now only stand by and watch as one tree after another ignited, like giant candles on a birthday cake.

After the eleven o'clock news, a fresh crew arrived, along with volunteers who had heard about the fire on television. Wearily, Elliot handed his hose over to someone else. As he turned, wiping his face with a handkerchief, he spotted Meera and her father relinquishing their rakes.

Startled, his eyes met hers. "You're safe!" he breathed, relief washing over him like the water over the now smoldering cabin.

With one hand, Meera reached up to brush away a strand

of hair. She couldn't believe what she was seeing. He had tried to save her cabin. . .after all she'd done. . . .

Then he looked from her soot-streaked face to the astonished gaze of Bruce Briskin. "Maxwell?"

Abruptly, Elliot turned away, pretending not to hear. He was too exhausted to deal with a Briskin at a time like this.

Walking toward his own property line, he saw his mom and dad standing near the boulders, talking to the fire marshal. Soon afterward, the marshal announced over the speaker that any firefighters going off duty were welcome to shower and change at Chestnut Lodge. And there was plenty of food for everyone!

Soon tired, smoke-blackened workers were crossing the creek and heading for the lodge.

She and her father would not be among that number, of course, Meera thought as she watched them go. But she was startled when her father interrupted her musings. "I owe that boy an apology," Bruce Briskin said, staring after Elliot. "Years ago, I got into a fight with his dad in front of him. The guilt over that has never left me. No wonder he despises me."

"It's not you, Daddy. It's me! I made a mess of everything! He. . .hates me!" Meera blurted, unable to meet her father's inquiring's gaze.

"If that's so, he has a strange way of showing it," he remarked solemnly. "The boy risks his life by trespassing on Briskin property, puts his men to work saving land that, according to you, he knows will not be offered to him but might be sold to a developer, and spends hours protecting Briskin property when his own is in no imminent danger."

He put his arm around his daughter, and she nestled her head against his shoulder. "Suppose I should thank the Maxwells personally," he mused. "Maybe even offer to sell the mountain to them."

"Oh, Daddy!" she wailed and he held her closer.

"That should make you happy," he said. "Isn't that what you wanted all along?" He tilted her chin upward with his finger and looked into her face.

Meera nodded gratefully.

"Maybe you should thank him too, honey. It's your property—your cabin he tried to save."

❧

It was a small fire by forest standards, not much more than a brushfire, they said later when the assessment had been made and only four hundred acres were found to have been burned. By now all the firefighters were gone, except for the few who would linger until the rains came.

After it was all over, Max Maxwell consented to see Bruce Briskin. And promptly at nine A.M. the next morning, Briskin walked through the doors of Chestnut Lodge. He wore a dark suit and tie, and every hair on his silvery head was in place.

"Good morning," he said politely.

Elliot nodded. "Come this way, please," he said, leading the way to his father's office.

Although Max offered the man a seat, he remained standing, as did Elliot, who waited with his arms folded across his chest.

Despite the fact that Briskin had praised the Maxwells publicly for preventing what might have been a disastrous forest fire, Elliot was not convinced of the man's sincerity. Privately he might say something to upset his father, and Elliot was determined to be present in case he had to escort Briskin out of the office.

But to their utter amazement, Briskin thanked them once again, explaining that the investigation had shown the explosion had been caused by a gasoline container. Elias Briskin had kept it under the back porch for his chain saw, and apparently over time, the plastic lid had melted, allowing noxious fumes to escape. There was also evidence that someone had smoked a cigarette while sitting on the back steps. When questioned, one of the surveyors admitted that he had smoked but was fairly certain he'd dropped the stub in a glass of lemonade. But everyone knew it took only the flick of an ash to kindle a fire among the dry leaves.

"The mountain adjacent to your property is for sale," he went on. "It's yours if you wish to purchase it—a prime parcel."

"We'll check it out, of course," Max said guardedly.

Briskin colored. "I understand. Guess I can't blame you for not taking my word for it."

"I'll leave the final decision to my son." Max nodded toward Elliot, whose stance had not changed. "You'll have to deal with him now."

"Then you're the man I need to see," Briskin said, pausing. "I have a score to settle with you."

Elliot waited for what he suspected had been coming all along. But he was bowled over when, instead of condemning him for his conduct with Meera, the man apologized instead for the fight staged in Elliot's presence on that long-ago afternoon. "Now. . .my daughter would like to speak to you too. She would have come with me, but she feels she would not be welcome here."

Elliot's startled expression told Bruce all he needed to know, so he added, "She's down at the cabin, assessing the damage."

twelve

Elliot paused at the boulders that bordered Turkey Creek, seeing the devastation on the other side. Where the Briskin cabin had once stood proudly was now only a blackened stone chimney and a few twisted, charred objects, scarcely identifiable.

Scanning the mountainside, he saw burned stumps and scorched tree trunks, shorn of their limbs. He and the others might have managed to save a forest, but the vale was a black hole, lifeless and dark. The firefighters had gone. There was nothing left to fight. No fire smoldered in the gray ashes.

But Elliot felt keenly the unseasonably warm day when he spotted the hood of a silver convertible winking in the sun far up the road. Then she emerged from the trees. Despite his knowledge that she might be married, his blood sang at the sight of her. She was wearing a simple T-shirt and blue jeans, but she had never looked lovelier to him. A cloud of silver-blond hair fell around her shoulders, catching the glint of the sunlight that filtered through the trees.

With her head down, she appeared wistful, moving forlornly along the path, scuffing the scorched earth with the toe of her tennis shoe. He could only imagine what she must be feeling.

❧

Meera had been watching for what seemed like hours, wondering if her dad had lost his courage and decided not to show up at Chestnut Lodge after all. Or maybe Elliot and his father had turned him away. Still, she wished she could see Elliot once more, if only to thank him again for trying to save the cabin. Who would have thought a Maxwell would have done that for a Briskin!

When she saw a jeaned figure approaching, she stopped her aimless pacing and watched as he hopped effortlessly across the rocks and strode resolutely along the creek bank toward her. The breeze, smelling of burned wood, lifted his curls and tossed them across his forehead. His tan had deepened during the summer, she noticed. And when he stood in front of her, she saw that his knit shirt was the exact color of his deep blue eyes.

He read the profound loss in her glance, then turned to follow her gaze toward the chimney.

"I'm so sorry," Elliot said, seeing the sad spectacle. "We did all we could to save it."

"You and your men saved the forest, Elliot. Perhaps even the Briskin home. Thank you. . .so much."

"I only wish we could have done more. But you could build another cabin someday. . .in your grandfather's memory."

Meera stared at the charred landscape and sighed. "It wouldn't be the same."

Respecting her grief, he waited. "This may be little consolation, Meera, but losing this piece of land to a fire has brought our families closer than they have been in generations."

Even you and me, Elliot? she yearned to ask. Her hair swung about her shoulders as she turned her imploring, smoky eyes to his, and her voice trembled uncertainly. "Maybe. . . this could be made into a little haven in memory of *both* our grandfathers, who were the best of friends. . .once."

Elliot lifted his gaze toward the distant mountain peak. He had thought the clearing might be left to grow wild, erasing any memory of Meera, thus easing his pain. Now, with a glance toward heaven, his excitement began to build. Some good could come from this, after all, and she would not be completely lost to him. "I like that. We could turn this spot into a place of. . .love and friendship."

Meera ran a few steps ahead and turned, stirring puffs of ash along the path. The sun, rising higher, sparked her gray eyes with blue. "Guests could come here from Chestnut Lodge. Families could bring their children." She brightened. "You don't have a children's park at the lodge, do you?"

"No," he said, delighted with the idea. "And our own children could play here."

Our children? She stared at him. Saw him grimace as if he'd said the wrong thing. He scuffed his shoe in the ash which settled as gray dust on the toe of his white tennis shoe.

Meera caught her breath and dared to test it. "I couldn't very well have children without getting married first," she quipped. "Unless I wanted to start another family feud."

"Let's don't do that," he countered. "We've just begun to work this one out."

She moved to face him. "I'm sorry for all the trouble I caused you, Elliot. But I didn't know how else to approach you."

He reached over and took her hand. "Your approach was quite unforgettable," he replied and finally looked from her shining eyes to her hand. There was no ring on her finger. No white circle. "Do you know why I was so upset with you the night of the storm?"

She ducked her head, feeling the heat stain her cheeks a becoming shade of pink. He gently lifted her chin with his finger. "Because I was afraid I could never have you. That you were going to marry that guy and I'd never see you again. Never hold you. Never kiss you."

"Oh, Elliot, I feel the same way. It started the moment we met. Then you turned out to be one of those unscrupulous Maxwells." She giggled.

He searched her face, her eyes, and could hardly believe

what he saw there. "You're. . .no longer engaged?"

"I returned Clark's ring as soon as I reached Venezuela."

Afraid to believe the joy that began to engulf him, he stomped about in mock disgust, raising the dust. "So you let me sweat it out all summer!"

Her voice was soft with wonder. "I thought you. . .despised me."

Ignoring any apprehension, he said sincerely, "Without you, there's a constant ache in my heart."

"Oh, Elliot, I thought you didn't want me. You said it was a game."

"How could you believe that?"

She shrugged. "How could our grandfathers have believed such terrible things about each other?"

"I think," he said, moving nearer, "it's time we put this animosity behind us."

"You mean. . .start over?"

"I mean. . .take up where we left off."

"Oh," she said in a small voice. She brushed her hair back from her face and looked toward the creek. "We could build a bridge across the creek so people won't have to rock-hop or wade through."

"Good idea, Meera." His enthusiasm grew. "There's an old shed on our property made of American chestnut wood. We've talked about tearing it down, but it has symbolized our heritage and how we've built on the loss of the forest. We can use those boards across the bridge and make a wooden railing above the stone. That will be *my* grandfather's contribution."

"Oh, Elliot," she breathed, "don't you think our grandfathers are hearing us. . .and approve?"

"Without a doubt," he said staunchly, "Jonas Maxwell is the one who put the bug in the ear of the Lord to bring us together."

"Oh, you!" she teased, hitting him playfully on the arm. "If anybody, it's Elias Briskin. He's the one who wanted to make peace all along."

"My foot!" Elliot exclaimed. "He came to the house on my grandfather's wedding day so he could try to get his girl back!" He looked down into her upturned face, so close to his, and grew serious. "But when a Maxwell marries a woman, he's not going to let her get away."

"I don't want to get away, Elliot."

He smiled down at her. "Our home will be built on the Word of God, Meera, and faith in the One who created this fantastic beauty. Let's always obey that greatest commandment of Jesus. . .to love one another."

She nodded. Then an impish look crossed her face, and she could not contain the sparkle in her eyes. "There's something I've been wanting to do. I've always wanted to stand on the Briskin side of the creek and put my big toe in the Maxwell side. . .without falling down, that is."

A wide grin spread over his face. "And there's something I've wanted to do for the past ten years. Let's go!"

He grabbed her hand and ran with her to the creek, sitting down on the bank to take off their shoes and socks. Meera waded in until the water was up to her knees. Balancing herself, the water flowing around her, she lifted one leg and planted her foot on the other side. Then, lifting her arms in victory, she threw back her head and shouted as the warm sun caressed her face.

Elliot waded in to stand beside her. "How does it feel?"

"Brrr! It's cold!" She shivered. "But exhilarating!" A frown wrinkled her smooth brow. "But. . ."

"But what?" Elliot asked.

"It's not quite the same as when I was a little girl,

challenging the Maxwells with a song Louisa and I made up while trembling uncontrollably, pretending it was only because of the cold creek water."

"Well," he said, rubbing his jaw, a strange glitter appearing in his eyes, "*your* childhood dream has at least been realized. You did stick your toe on the Maxwell side of the creek. Now, it's my turn. There's something I need to get off my chest."

"Then do it," she encouraged him.

"All right, I will!" he said and with that he reached out, scooped up the startled Meera in his arms, and deposited her smack dab on the Briskin side of the creek.

Mouth agape, she sat up, the icy water creeping up to her chest, and stared at him.

He moved back and shouted, "I wouldn't dare touch you, Meera Briskin! Not even with a ten-foot pole!"

"Po—le. . .po—le. . .po-le" echoed in the still forest.

Then Meera remembered. "That was. . .*you*?" she shrieked.

"Yooooooo! . . .ooooo. . .ooooo!" bounced back to them from the Maxwell/Briskin Mountains. Their laughter rang through the hills and surrounded them with joy.

She began to scoop up the water and fling it at him, but he didn't back away. Instead, he came closer and dropped down beside her, sitting in the Maxwell side of the creek. Then he pulled her to him, and they sat shivering on the Maxwell-Briskin property line. "Elliot," she said on a quivery breath, "I was wrong in what I said years ago." His look of love encouraged her to continue. "Life doesn't have to consist of feudin,' fussin,' and fightin'. . .to be excitin.'"

In acknowledgment, he lowered his dark head to her silvery one and their lips began silently, but profoundly, proving that point, while the laughing waters of the creek flowed around them.

A Letter To Our Readers

Dear Reader:

In order that we might better contribute to your reading enjoyment, we would appreciate your taking a few minutes to respond to the following questions. When completed, please return to the following:

Rebecca Germany, Editor
Heartsong Presents
P.O. Box 719
Uhrichsville, Ohio 44683

1. Did you enjoy reading *Mountain Man*?
   ❑ Very much. I would like to see more books
       by this author!
   ❑ Moderately
       I would have enjoyed it more if _____

   _____

2. Are you a member of *Heartsong Presents*? Yes   No
   If no, where did you purchase this book? _____

   _____

3. What influenced your decision to purchase this
   book? (Check those that apply.)

   ❑ Cover   ❑ Back cover copy
   ❑ Title   ❑ Friends
   ❑ Publicity   ❑ Other _____

4. On a scale from 1 (poor) to 10 (superior), please rate
   the following elements.

   ___Heroine   ___Plot

   ___Hero   ___Inspirational theme

   ___Setting   ___Secondary characters

5. What settings would you like to see covered in
   Heartsong Presents books?

   _____

   _____

6. What are some inspirational themes you would like
   to see treated in future books?_____

   _____

   _____

7. Would you be interested in reading other *Heartsong
   Presents* titles?   ❑ Yes   ❑ No

8. Please check your age range:
   ❑ Under 18   ❑ 18-24   ❑ 25-34
   ❑ 35-45   ❑ 46-55   ❑ Over 55

9. How many hours per week do you read? ————

Name _____

Occupation _____

Address _____

City _____ State _____ Zip _____

Contemporary Inspirational Romance From

Yvonne Lehman

___*Drums of Shelomoh*—As a nurse, Crystal Janis has seen it all. That is, until her visit to a mission outpost in Rhodesia, Africa. A much-needed vacation becomes a series of challenging crises and a chance for lasting love. HP37 $2.95

___*Southern Gentleman*—When Norah Brown's sister and Thornton Winter's brother die in a tragic accident, they leave behind their baby daughter, Camille. Norah and Thornton are both determined to raise the child in their own way. What will it take to bridge the wide ocean between them—for Camille's sake, as well as their own? HP82 $2.95

___*Mountain Man*—Meera Briskin is determined to find out for herself whether the Maxwells are the unmitigated rogues she has been taught to hate. Posing as a participant at a writer's conference held at the famous Chestnut Lodge, run by none other than Elliot Maxwell, Meera soon finds herself caught in the web of her own deception. HP126 $2.95

┅┅┅┅┅ Hearts♥ng ┅┅┅┅┅

Any 12 *Heartsong Presents* titles for only $26.95 *

CONTEMPORARY ROMANCE IS CHEAPER BY THE DOZEN!

Buy any assortment of twelve *Heartsong Presents* titles and save 25% off of the already discounted price of $2.95 each!

*plus $1.00 shipping and handling per order and sales tax where applicable.

HEARTSONG PRESENTS TITLES AVAILABLE NOW:

__HP 3 RESTORE THE JOY, *Sara Mitchell*
__HP 4 REFLECTIONS OF THE HEART, *Sally Laity**
__HP 5 THIS TREMBLING CUP, *Marlene Chase*
__HP 6 THE OTHER SIDE OF SILENCE, *Marlene Chase*
__HP 9 HEARTSTRINGS, *Irene B. Brand**
__HP 10 SONG OF LAUGHTER, *Lauraine Snelling**
__HP 13 PASSAGE OF THE HEART, *Kjersti Hoff Baez*
__HP 14 A MATTER OF CHOICE, *Susannah Hayden*
__HP 18 LLAMA LADY, *VeraLee Wiggins**
__HP 19 ESCORT HOMEWARD, *Eileen M. Berger**
__HP 21 GENTLE PERSUASION, *Veda Boyd Jones*
__HP 22 INDY GIRL, *Brenda Bancroft*
__HP 25 REBAR, *Mary Carpenter Reid*
__HP 26 MOUNTAIN HOUSE, *Mary Louise Colln*
__HP 29 FROM THE HEART, *Sara Mitchell*
__HP 30 A LOVE MEANT TO BE, *Brenda Bancroft*
__HP 33 SWEET SHELTER, *VeraLee Wiggins*
__HP 34 UNDER A TEXAS SKY, *Veda Boyd Jones*
__HP 37 DRUMS OF SHELOMOH, *Yvonne Lehman*
__HP 38 A PLACE TO CALL HOME, *Eileen M. Berger*
__HP 41 FIELDS OF SWEET CONTENT, *Norma Jean Lutz*
__HP 42 SEARCH FOR TOMORROW, *Mary Hawkins*
__HP 45 DESIGN FOR LOVE, *Janet Gortsema*
__HP 46 THE GOVERNOR'S DAUGHTER, *Veda Boyd Jones*
__HP 49 YESTERDAY'S TOMORROWS, *Linda Herring*
__HP 50 DANCE IN THE DISTANCE, *Kjersti Hoff Baez*
__HP 53 MIDNIGHT MUSIC, *Janelle Burnham*
__HP 54 HOME TO HER HEART, *Lena Nelson Dooley*
__HP 57 LOVE'S SILKEN MELODY, *Norma Jean Lutz*
__HP 58 FREE TO LOVE, *Doris English*
__HP 61 PICTURE PERFECT, *Susan Kirby*
__HP 62 A REAL AND PRECIOUS THING, *Brenda Bancroft*
__HP 65 ANGEL FACE, *Frances Carfi Matranga*
__HP 66 AUTUMN LOVE, *Ann Bell*
__HP 69 BETWEEN LOVE AND LOYALTY, *Susannah Hayden*

*Temporarily out of stock.

(If ordering from this page, please remember to include it with the order form.)

········· Presents ·········

__HP 70 A NEW SONG, *Kathleen Yapp*
__HP 73 MIDSUMMER'S DREAM, *Rena Eastman*
__HP 74 SANTANONI SUNRISE, *Hope Irvin Marston and Claire M. Coughlin*
__HP 77 THE ROAD BEFORE ME, *Susannah Hayden*
__HP 78 A SIGN OF LOVE, *Veda Boyd Jones* *
__HP 81 BETTER THAN FRIENDS, *Sally Laity*
__HP 82 SOUTHERN GENTLEMEN, *Yvonne Lehman*
__HP 85 LAMP IN DARKNESS, *Connie Loraine*
__HP 86 POCKETFUL OF LOVE, *Loree Lough*
__HP 89 CONTAGIOUS LOVE, *Ann Bell*
__HP 90 CATER TO A WHIM, *Norma Jean Lutz*
__HP 93 IDITAROD DREAM, *Janelle Jamison*
__HP 94 TO BE STRONG, *Carolyn R. Scheidies*
__HP 97 A MATCH MADE IN HEAVEN, *Kathleen Yapp*
__HP 98 BEAUTY FOR ASHES, *Becky Melby and Cathy Wienke*
__HP101 DAMAGED DREAMS, *Mary Hawkins*
__HP102 IF GIVEN A CHOICE, *Tracie J. Peterson*
__HP105 CIRCLE OF LOVE, *Alma Blair*
__HP106 RAGDOLL, *Kelly R. Stevens*
__HP109 INSPIRED LOVE, *Ann Bell*
__HP110 CALLIE'S MOUNTAIN, *Veda Boyd Jones*
__HP113 BETWEEN THE MEMORY AND THE MOMENT, *Susannah Hayden*
__HP114 THE QUIET HEART, *Rae Simons*
__HP117 FARTHER ALONG THE ROAD, *Susannah Hayden*
__HP118 FLICKERING FLAMES, *Connie Loraine*
__HP121 THE WINNING HEART, *Norma Jean Lutz*
__HP122 THERE'S ALWAYS TOMORROW, *Brenda Bancroft*
__HP125 LOVE'S TENDER GIFT, *Elizabeth Murphy*
__HP126 MOUNTAIN MAN, *Yvonne Lehman*   *Temporarily out of stock.

Great Inspirational Romance at a Great Price!

Heartsong Presents books are inspirational romances in contemporary and historical settings, designed to give you an enjoyable, spirit-lifting reading experience. You can choose from 128 wonderfully written titles from some of today's best authors like Colleen L. Reece, Brenda Bancroft, Janelle Jamison, and many others.

When ordering quantities less than twelve, above titles are $2.95 each.